Books by Janet McNeill

TOM'S TOWER

THE BATTLE OF ST. GEORGE WITHOUT

GOODBYE, DOVE SQUARE

Goodbye,
Dove Square

Goodbye,
Dove Square

by Janet McNeill

Illustrated by
Mary Russon

Little, Brown and Company
BOSTON   TORONTO

LIBRARY OF CONGRESS CATALOG CARD NO. 69–11785

FIRST EDITION

PRINTED IN THE UNITED STATES OF AMERICA

Goodbye,
Dove Square

I

"THAT'S money, old son, just in case you're interested," Henry said, waving the open envelope under Matt's nose. "Lovely lolly, hard earned cash, that's what that is. And all belongs to yours truly."

"Very nice, too." Matt tried to make his voice sound casual, as if the sight of the crisp folded notes and the sound of unseen coins moving between Henry's finger and thumb didn't interest him very much.

"Every Friday, regular as manna," Henry said, "and after Christmas I'm due for a rise."

"I suppose you are." Matt knew that the words were a little bleak. He tried to count the edges of the pound notes without actually appearing to do so, but the hasty answer he arrived at seemed an impossible sum. Surely Henry didn't get as much as all that in Mr. Beddows' office? He'd only been there just over a year, left school one week and started work the next.

"Mind you I earn it," Henry continued, " 'The laborer is worthy of his hire.' " Although his voice had broken and he no longer sang in the Cathedral choir there were still traces of piety about his language, especially when he was happy or excited. Money, whether it was shillings earned as a chorister or pound notes paid to him by Mr. Beddows, never faiied to excite Henry and make him happy.

He pushed a plate across to Matt. "Have another doughnut, why don't you?"

"No, thanks," Matt said.

"Go on. Don't be a dope."

The doughnut tempted Matt with its dark, jammy eye. "Oh, all right. Thanks." Eating was one of the unfailing and perpetual pleasures. School dinner had been more than usually skimpy today, but he wished he hadn't bumped into Henry on the way home or accepted his invitation to this smooth Coffee Bar. In the old days he'd often blamed Henry for being mean in sharing out a Nuttycrunch or a bag of Crisps, but this kind of hospitality was equally unfair and Henry knew it.

Matt shoved his old duffle bag, stuffed full with textbooks, a little farther out of sight below the counter. "What sort of work do you actually do, Henry?"

Henry looked vague. "Oh — brewing tea," he said, "or taking telephone messages, or running errands for the boss (that's what I'm doing now, ha ha!) or licking stamps." He made a joke out of it since Matt would hardly understand the world of Big Business. "Very important stamps, of course." He shook two half crowns out of his wage packet and stowed the envelope in the pocket of his snazzy pants.

"How's school these days?" he asked, as if school was some half-forgotten joke that they'd once shared, a kind of folly dredged up from the misty memories of child-

4

hood. The new term had just started. Matt had been the only one staying on.

"School's all right."

"Same old grind?"

"More or less."

"Same old dreary fossils?"

"Drearier," Matt said, hating himself.

Henry laughed, and ran the flat of his palm lovingly over his long glossy hair. His fingernails, Matt noticed with shock, were even and clean. "Rather you than me," Henry said. "I don't know how you stick with it, honest. But then you always were one of the bright boys, weren't you?" He mocked Matt with the compliment. Matt chewed on his doughnut, determined not to let Henry spoil it for him.

"Going to the University, are you?"

"Wouldn't be surprised."

"Good old Matt." The way Henry said it it sounded like a pat for a dog. "By the way have you tried the ice rink down at the Amusement Center?"

"No. I haven't. Not yet. All right, is it?"

"Not bad at all," Henry said. "You should come along some night."

"Oh I don't know."

He did know, of course. He'd gone past the place, heard the music, seen through the open door the colored lights changing like a waltzing rainbow, watched people going in, putting down their five bob as if they were halfpennies. Another half crown for the hire of skates, the notice said. Of course Matt knew. And Henry knew, too.

"Saturday night's the best," Henry said. "You come along some Saturday."

"I've got exams coming up," Matt mumbled. He remembered sliding with Henry on patches of frozen pavement with someone standing at the corner to keep watch for a policeman, and the fierce excitement of speed combined with lawbreaking.

"Exams? I thought you'd passed everything there was to pass," Henry grinned.

"Not quite. Just give me time."

He wanted to push Henry's silly face in, but after two free doughnuts and a cup of Expresso this wasn't possible; in any case you couldn't do any face-pushing in this sort of a joint.

"Exams never bothered our Matt," Henry said.

They'd never bothered Henry either, thought Matt. The only difference had been that Henry rarely passed them. "Coming to the meeting this evening?" he asked, to change the subject.

"What meeting?"

"At the Community Center. Someone stuck a note under our door."

"What's it in aid of?"

"To do with the trees being slashed, the new ones they'd planted in front of the Flats."

"Bet you it was Gwen's note. She's always on about something."

"It isn't only Gwen, it's a lot of people. Anyway, I don't see it's funny, cutting the trees like that."

"Are you going?"

"Me? What do you think? Of course I'm not."

That was the strange thing. Matt had no intention of going to the meeting. Two years ago he'd have been there, pushing to get into the front row, ganging up like crazy, scheming with the rest of them to find out who had slashed the wispy little trees a couple of weeks after they had been so carefully planted, making a cause and a crusade out of it, plot and counterplot, nose to the ground, sleuthing for clues like puppy dogs. But not now. Not any more. Running around with a mob wasn't exciting the way it used to be. In any case it was all too much bother, like a lot of other things. Some idiot had taken his knife to those trees; it was no business of Matt's to find out who or why. It didn't fill him with indignation. It didn't matter much to him whether the shorn slopes of doubtful green in front of the Flats would have trees growing on them twenty years from now or whether they wouldn't. In any case, trees were not things that you planted out so many feet apart, and staked and labeled and waited for. Trees, trees that were really trees, were there before you were, established objects like mountains or grandparents or Christmas.

But something made him ask, "Do you remember those other trees?"

"What other trees?" asked Henry, his cheek swollen with doughnut.

"Idiot. You know. The trees in Dove Square."

Less than three years ago they had all been living in the great decaying giants of houses in Dove Square, down in the city, with the Church of St. George Without, smothered over by trees, at its center. Henry needn't pretend he'd forgotten.

"Oh — those trees. They'll be all cut down by this time." Henry was quite untroubled. "They go through them like butter with those big saws. Wheee!" He imitated the noise the big saws made on wood.

"Ever been back there?" Matt asked.

"No. Have you?"

"No," Matt said.

"Nothing to go for, really."

Matt, scraping the last of the wet sugar from the bottom of his cup, looked up and caught Henry's eye, and for a moment the dust of the Battle of St. George Without stirred between them. Then Henry's eyes glazed, refusing to admit childish memories.

"We're not kids any more," he said. "Well, I mean, are we?" He got up, clinking the two half crowns in his palm, and went to the counter to pay the girl. He stopped to talk to her, chatting her up a bit for Matt's benefit. Matt fished out his duffle bag and went and stood in the doorway with his school cap screwed up small in his hand. He didn't want to put it on till the last possible moment.

Henry joined him with a pleased expression on his face. "And remember, if you do change your mind about the ice rink — " he said.

"Well — thanks — if I do."

"Flat 157, B. Block, 5th Floor," Henry said.

"Thanks for the doughnuts anyway," Matt growled, guessing quickly which direction Henry was likely to take and choosing the opposite.

He had guessed right and was glad to have the pavement to himself. Now he would have to go back to the Flats by the long way, but he didn't mind.

"Hiya, Matt!" called a voice from the opposite pavement.

It was Sidney, the Jamaican boy, in his white painter's overalls and with a lunch box tucked under his arm.

"Hiya, Sidney! How's trade?"

"Most excellently profitable," Sidney called.

"Coming back to the Flats, are you?"

"Going to pick up my pay packet first. You be turning up this evening, will you?"

"Maybe," Matt said. Sidney played the guitar with a group at the Youth Club and had glossy ambitions.

"Sure is a good show, exceedingly slick and tuneful," Sidney called. "Lovely oompa. You come along."

Matt remembered seeing Sidney on a motorbike last Sunday. Anyway he was getting a sore throat from shouting. "Well, maybe," he said, and moved off.

A gaggle of girls from the grammar school were waiting at the bus stop, making silly remarks to each other in their genteel voices. "Oh, Mavis — you didn't really say that — not to Her!" "I did — honest!" Mavis declared. They squealed "Gosh!" and widened their eyes.

One of them a little apart from the others was strok-

ing the pavement with the tips of her shoes in a kind of
private half-dance. As Matt went by she turned suddenly, and her long straight hair, like seaweed, swung
into his face. If he'd been a little quicker off the mark
he would have caught hold of it and yanked, but he
missed his chance. He heard them giggling shrilly, and
when he had gone a few steps farther he let a piercing
whistle out between his teeth, and laughed in a rude,
hollow way without turning to look at their pink, indignant faces.

He was in no hurry at all to go home. The row of

lighted shopwindows drew him toward them. In the stationer's, the fireworks that had not been sold by Guy Fawkes night were piled haphazard against the window, at bargain prices. Fireworks no longer tempted him, though he remembered how friendly a Catherine wheel warm from his pocket used to smell. The chemist's window, anticipating Christmas, was full of small, velvet-lined boxes with soap and perfume and lipstick and bath cubes and hand cream bedded in them. He eyed the price tickets, judging whether out of his pocket money he would be able to raise enough to buy one of the larger boxes for his mother. She would gasp and say, "Oh, how lovely! Oh, Matt — but you shouldn't!" and when the box had been sufficiently admired she would slide it into a drawer. In some curious way she would be pleased with the gift, although he didn't know what she did with the stuff afterwards, apart from the soap. Probably Henry would be aiming at the biggest box of the lot, a great vulgar slab of pale blue trimmed with satin bows, to present to some girl at the ice rink. She wouldn't stow it away in a drawer.

There were eight shops in a row, one of each kind, and there was also the cleaner's, the post office, the baby clinic, the Youth Club (Sidney's photograph prominent on the board outside), the Community Center, the Senior Citizens' Reading Room and the library. Everything matched everything else. Everything was new, glossy, tidy, convenient. In front of him now rose the four great blocks of the Flats, like cliffs, presiding. Come on, they seemed to say, come on home to your comfortable, centrally heated, amenity-crammed, labor-saving little hutch with its Meccano-scale balcony, come on in like everybody else and enjoy yourself. Pop your litter into your litter basket and your rubbish down your rubbish chute and forget about them. Take great deep breaths of air from this smokeless zone. You lucky people, here is the Happy Land, not Far Far Away like it used to be but right at hand, Specially Tailored for You. Whatever you want you name it — we've got it.

You have, have you, Matt thought with that uneasy uncomforted feeling inside him. He didn't like the Flats. He didn't like their convenience and newness. He didn't like the way everything was handed out on a plate, so that whether you were having teething troubles or wanted to buy a couple of stamps or borrow a book or drink a pint or wash the clothes or choose a pork chop or listen to pop or complain about your rheumatism you could do it all, almost without thinking.

Outside the Community Center a board displayed a notice: TONIGHT — PROTEST MEETING. It seemed peculiar that in this paradise anything was left to protest about, but the hall would be packed to the doors tonight. In Dove Square, in the old days, people just put up with things and laughed or grumbled or shouted; here they formed themselves into committees and passed resolutions and protested. Gwen when she came off duty at the hospital (she was training to be a nurse) would undoubtedly be in the front row, getting briefed.

He went up in the lift to the ninth floor and let himself in at the door of his own flat — the same as all the other doors except for its number. There was a note from his mother to say she would be working late at Mr. Ricardo's restaurant and he was to get his own tea. Afterwards he was to go round to Mr. Flint's and see if he would come to change a washer.

Mr. Ricardo's restaurant had changed like everything else when the people who lived in and around Dove Square moved out to the Happy Land. Now that his business was in a select part of the city, he had put up a notice — RICARDO'S WINE AND DINE — and inside it was all carpet and tablecloths and electric candles and separate tables — no more ice cream wafers handed across the counter to tempt a dredging tongue, or fish and chips to carry home in fragrant newspaper soggy with vinegar. Matt's mother, Mrs. McGinley, wore a black dress to work and there were three waiters to help her.

Matt got his tea, bad-temperedly and awkwardly, knocking things over because everything in the kitchen was so small and so conveniently near to everything else. He perched on the mushroom-sized stool with his plate balanced on the shelf that pretended to be a table. He thought of the big, bare kitchen in Dove Square where the table was broad enough to sprawl across it, elbows spread, of the stove that roared or smoked and ate up the coal, and of the uneven bumps and hollows of the tiled floor. His school blazer felt tight and the knobs of his wrists stuck out below the edges of his cuffs. These days he always seemed to be a size larger than he expected, and the space that was called home seemed a couple of sizes smaller. If he stretched out his arms he could reach across this kitchen from wall to wall, touching with his fingertips the border of washable flowers of which his mother was so proud. No room here to prance or rampage, if you felt inclined that way. Hardly room to whistle or yawn. One of these days he would grow so large that he would split this place wide open, and then what?

He gobbled his food quickly, without chewing very much, and decided that he must get outside this little box and do some digesting in a place where there was space to digest in quiet decency.

Probably the man had been standing with his finger aimed at the bell at the very moment that Matt opened the door. Matt disentangled himself and discovered that the visitor was tall, and though his clothes were shabby there was a swagger about him, a tired elegance, an air of pleasantness, as if he was sure everyone would be very pleased to see him and quite right too.

Matt wasn't pleased. "What is it?"

"Can I have the pleasure of a word with the lady of the house?" Even while the man was speaking his smile didn't disappear.

"No. Mum's out."

The man sighed. "Ah. Out, is she? Too bad. When will she be back?"

"I don't know. What do you want?"

"Not what I want, lad," the man said, "it's what *she* wants." He held out a large leather case and unzipped it. Words came from him like toothpaste out of a tube and he held up one object after another.

"A quality product, lad — you're not too young to recognize quality when you see it — geared to the pace of modern living, that goes without saying — science in the kitchen, let knowledge work for *you* — intelligence teamed with imagination — who wants to slice eggs the way Grannie sliced eggs? — admire its sleek design, its versatility — dicing carrots, adjust this blade — bread crumbs? nothing simpler — and for coring apples, well I'm glad you asked about that — this little gadget here — the work of a moment."

"If you're selling something, then we don't want any," Matt said.

Probably the man hadn't heard him; he dived into his case again. "The fragrance of a summer cloud in your own home," he said. "Dispels odor instantly, a thousand flowers burst into bloom at the touch of a button — easily operated — a child could use it."

"No," Matt said.

The man dived again. "So soft," he said, "so subtly supersoft. You have never imagined softness like this."

"No," Matt said.

The man leaned forward; the smile became more grim, more full of teeth. "Do you realize that statistics prove there are more serious accidents under the shelter of your own roof each year than on the motorways in the rush hour? The housewife never knows when disaster may strike. Burns, cuts, scalds, stings, falls, shocks — this little handbook tells you What to Do and When to Do It."

"I told you. No."

The man eyed him sadly. "Pity. Pity. I like to see people happy."

"They are happy," Matt said, "with Green Stamps and Pink Stamps and Tuppence Off and Bargain Offers and Coupons and their kitchens stuffed with things for chopping and peeling and coring and dicing and grating and everything wipe-clean and drip dry. And Bingo and the Pools and Adult Education and the telly," he finished rather lamely.

Now the man had stooped again and was lifting smaller objects out of his case, handling them tenderly. There were little brooches in every imaginable shape and color, long necklaces of pearls gleaming gently, earrings that swung and glittered, sending out needles of blue light, impossibly small watches purring busily like a company of contented kittens.

"Christmas coming up," he said. "You'll be looking for a present for your mother, I daresay."

"Maybe I will."

There was one watch with a face like a daisy. It caught Matt's eye and held it. There was something irresistible about its smallness, it was so impossibly small; the hands were like frozen hairs.

"You won't get a chance like this in the shops," the man said, "not at this price."

"Even so I haven't the money."

"Pity. Pity." He was holding the watch in his palm, admiring it.

Matt growled, "I'm still at school."

"Ah well, there it is." The man knelt to put the treasures back in his case. "Not long now till they let you out. That'll be the day, eh?" He straightened up. "Nice place you've got here."

"It's all right."

Matt's voice betrayed his lack of enthusiasm. "What's the matter with it, lad? Don't you like it here?" the man asked.

Matt said, "Not as much as — " and stopped.

"As where?"

"As where we used to live."

"And where was that?"

Something, some sense of sudden warning, a faint alarm bell, a red light flickering from a long way off, pulled Matt up sharply, and he said, "Oh — down in the city."

"Been moved out, have you?"

"Yes."

"I heard they'd cleared a lot of the old houses," the Salesman said.

"That's right. They're pulling them down. They said they weren't worth repairing."

"Whole center of the city has changed since my time — hardly knew it — houses down on all sides. I had friends who used to live about the center of the city, a kind of square it was, trees in the middle. Tried to look them up but the place was altered so much I couldn't be sure where I was. Maybe you could help me. Maybe you came from a place like that — a square with trees?"

"Ours was a street," Matt lied. "Just a plain street, no trees or grass for miles," and he slammed the door of the flat behind him and made for the stairs, unwilling, for no reason that he could have explained, to share his past or the lift with this stranger.

2

WHEN Matt had dawdled down nine flights of stairs and come out into the open air he was glad to see there was no sign of the Salesman. The pavements were crowded with people who had had their meal and were now setting off like cheerful and obedient sheep to do the things that the planners of the Happy Land had decided they would want to do in the evenings. Behind him the dark faces of the Flats were studded with lighted windows.

Matt decided that the thing he most wanted to do was to get away from it all. If he could find somewhere untidy and private and inconvenient, somewhere that reminded him of the way things used to be, somewhere established and shabby, a place that had grown and wasn't Specially Tailored for him or for anybody else, he might come back in a better temper. Tonight his homework would have to wait. He could do his errand with Pa Flint on the way home.

He waited until the crowd had thinned a little — until the protesters and the pop fans and the people with dirty washing and the cinema queue had all fed themselves into the slots that were provided for them —

and then he shinned the high wall at the end of the road and dropped the eight feet into the rough grass of the old railway cutting. Few trains now ran on this line; there was talk of the line being closed altogether. Some of the windows in the little station had had stones put through them; others were boarded up. Below the high arch of stonework where the road passed over the railway, the sides of the cutting were steeply sloped. The grass was long and matted, the growth of many summers, and bushes which had grown from seeds blown from back gardens years and years ago tore at his legs. A roosting bird, disturbed, went up squawking. He saw its wings black against the pattern of city roofs and chimneys and steeples. Below him the blue steel ribbons of the railway lines curved into the distance. There was a comfortable railway smell in the air.

Matt felt better and found a place for himself, where he could squat with his heels rammed into a solid hummock of coarse grass and his backbone cunningly adjusted to the slope. He pulled a stalk and chewed it, whistling breathily.

He had whistled the tune through three times when he knew without moving that someone as well as himself was hearing it. He finished the tune through once more before he turned his head.

"Hallo you."

It was Madge. His eyes separated her from the shadow of the bush against which she was sitting.

"What are you doing snooping?" he asked.

"I was here before you were. I watched you coming over the wall."

"Then you were snooping."

"Unless I'd had my eyes shut," she said, "I couldn't have helped seeing, could I?"

"What are you doing here, anyway?"

Madge shrugged and didn't look at him. She was sitting with her knees drawn up to her chin and her

shoulders humped. Her long red hair ran down to her shoes; even in the half-dark you felt its color.

Matt said, "You're getting spiders in your hair," but Madge said, "I like spiders," and dredged about in the grass with the tails of her hair, inviting visitors.

Matt took another look at her. "And you're all dolled up."

"So what?" Madge growled.

He could see she was wearing a bracelet and some beads, and a dress of flowery material showed under her coat. Her hair was shinier than usual and he thought she had been doing things to her face.

"What's the idea?" he asked. "Whatever are you like that for?"

"It's Cousin Maudie." Cousin Maudie was the weird cousin Madge lived with.

"What's Cousin Maudie on about?"

"It's the dance at the Youth Club. That's where she thinks I am."

"Well, why aren't you?"

"Have you ever been?"

"Me? No."

"You wouldn't ask if you had. All that giggle and being jolly in corners and the girls that have come with a boy queening it around and pretending they aren't sorry for you."

"So you come here instead."

"On Fridays," she said. "I like it here."

"It's all right."

They sat in silence staring at the sky. Above their heads it was crowded darkly by clouds, but over the heart of the city there was a pink luminous glow.

"Sitting by the wall smiling and praying hard that someone is going to pick you up," Madge said, "as if they were doing you a favor or something. All long hair and big feet and hot hands."

"Well, don't you get picked up?"

"Not me. Gwen does, though. All the time. You ought to see."

"Why don't you tell Cousin Maudie?"

"You can't tell her anything. Anyway she thinks — "

"What does she think?"

Madge imitated Cousin Maudie's voice. " 'You meet ever such a nice class of boy at the Youth Club.' " She sucked the end of one of the strands of hair, then spat it out.

"How long have you been here?"

"Not very long. I had to go down to the telly shop with Sammy."

Sammy was the youngest of the Flint family. Matt hardly knew the junior Flints except as a tribe of assorted sizes in assorted jerseys, all with pale flat hair. There still seemed to be as many of them as ever, although several of the older boys had left home. Madge of course knew their names and all about them and often had a youngster in tow.

"What did Sammy want to go to the telly shop for?"

Madge explained. Sammy wanted to see an installment of a television serial. The hire-purchase people had taken the Flint family's telly away, but the set in the window of the shop was turned on and they'd watched it from the pavement.

"Why do you have to go with him? He's old enough to go by himself."

"Yes, but he needs someone to watch it with."

"Why?"

Madge explained. Sammy was frightened if he

watched it by himself. He didn't like the serial; it gave him bad dreams.

"Then why on earth watch it?"

"If he doesn't, he says it's worse imagining."

"What was it this week?"

"Hands with no bodies holding daggers," Madge said, "and a death ray."

A solitary engine was coming down the track. The ground below them announced it before it arrived. The sound of it swallowed their voices. Long after it had passed they could still hear and smell it.

"How do you understand what that kid says?" Matt asked. Sammy talked in a funny kind of high-pitched gabble from which it was difficult to distinguish words or sense.

Madge prickled at once. "People are idiots. If they'd listen to him they'd understand."

"I can't," Matt said. "Not a word."

"Then that's your silly fault."

"He's a bit dim all round, isn't he? That's what they say at school anyway."

"Of course he isn't dim."

"I'm only telling you what they say."

There was a long silence. Madge's private death ray was directed at Matt. He stood it as long as he could; then he said, "I've got to call round at the Flints on my way back."

"What for?"

"Mum wants Mr. Flint to come and fix a washer."

"Then you needn't bother. He couldn't come anyway."

"Why couldn't he come?"

"When he gets back from work he's busy at home. Ma Flint has walked out."

"She's — what?"

"Walked out on him. Hopped it."

The way Madge said it, as if it were something ordinary, roused Matt as much as what she said. Girls were like that, he'd noticed, behaving as if they were used to things like this.

"She's done it before, you know," Madge said in an Auntie Madge kind of way.

"Has she?" Matt couldn't keep the shocked surprise out of his voice.

"Oh, you must have known, Matt." Madge sounded cross and impatient. "The trouble with you, Matt, is you have such a lovely nature. They were always rowing — at least she was. Even back in Dove Square. You must remember."

"I don't."

"You never notice anything!"

"The walls were thicker in Dove Square," Matt said, feeling embarrassed. "Anyway, why?"

Madge said, "Well, it's obvious." He didn't like to ask her to explain. He thought of Pa Flint, a small meek little man, always in the background, obscured by his enormous tired wife and that riot of boys. They didn't seem likely figures for a domestic drama.

"I suppose she'll come back," he said a little timidly. Madge agreed that she would, sometime. She always had before.

"I think it's awful," he hazarded, wishing she wouldn't take it so casually.

Madge said, "The thing about you, Matt, is you've got all your relations. You think everybody else should."

"My dad's dead."

"Yes, but you've got your mum, and uncles and aunts and grandfathers and cousins and things. Haven't you?"

"Back in the country. Dozens of them. But we hardly ever see them."

"All the same they're there. I haven't got anyone, only Cousin Maudie."

"Surely you know — "

"Not a thing except that my dad skipped it and didn't come back."

"Your mum, then?"

Madge didn't answer but he saw her shrug.

"You must know," he pressed. "Somebody must have said something back in Dove Square."

"They didn't. People in Dove Square took things the way they were."

For a brief moment he tried to imagine Madge as a tragic figure, the Orphan in the Storm, but it was no use, she didn't fit. A swaddled infant parked on a doorstep with the snowflakes falling thickly on its face. He looked sideways at Madge. She had become a dark shape. Only her breath, whitening in the night air, moved.

"It isn't a thing you go around asking about," she said. "Anyway, it never seemed to matter."

He thought it should have mattered, and said, "You could have asked Cousin Maudie."

"I used to sometimes."

"What did she say?"

"That I ought to be grateful." He heard her chuckling softly. "Or else she blew her top."

Cousin Maudie's top, he remembered, had always made sensational blowing.

"One time she cried," Madge said unexpectedly. "Bawled her head off. All her makeup rolled down onto the floor. I suppose it was funny, really. She was laying new linoleum in the kitchen — it was when we lived in Dove Square. The linoleum had daffodils and bunches of ribbon all over it, and she couldn't get it to fit. She was putting newspapers under it because of the damp coming up from the floor. I went on at her to tell me, but I knew she wasn't listening. I went on and on, just for spite, really, pretending I minded. And then I saw she was crying. I thought it was a joke at first but she wouldn't stop."

"What did you do?"

"I got scared and hopped it till she'd cooled off."

"Did she say anything afterwards?"

"Not a squeak. When I got back she'd gone out, it was her Bingo night. Next day she dyed her hair a different color and bought herself a new rig."

Matt felt angry with her for not minding. This was a

thing people should mind about. Perhaps she was pretending; you never knew with Madge. "All the same she ought to have told you, she must know something. Don't you remember anything about your mum and dad?"

"Not a thing."

"Have you tried?"

It had begun to rain. High above their heads, where the streetlights shone over the top of the wall, they could see the rain, like fine threads that seemed to hang.

Madge heaved herself to her feet. "Oh don't go on, Matt. I don't see the use of family trees. It's much less bother when people don't matter too much."

"All the same I think it's pretty lousy," he grumbled, and got up, rubbing the stiffness out of his knees.

"I shouldn't wonder if I'm a long-lost heiress," Madge said, teasing.

"If you were, then somebody would have bothered about you before this," Matt snapped, and was sorry at once. "Where are you going?"

The rain had thickened into rods and fell on the grass, hissing.

"Come on!" Madge cried. "The station — run for it!"

Stumbling and sliding, their ankles braced to the slope, their feet finding no sure purchase in the grassy tufts, with the rain now hammering on their heads and shoulders, they reached the station at last and found refuge in the little waiting room. The windows were smashed, or boarded up. The place smelled of age-old dust and tobacco. An advertisement embellished by

30

many amateur artists hung crooked from the peeling wall. Matt shook himself and heard the drops of water falling on the boards of the floor. Madge's hair swung in wet swathes.

"We'll have to wait till it eases," he said.

"It's too early for me to go back anyway, the dance doesn't end till eleven. Then I'll tell Cousin Maudie what a lovely time I had."

Madge made faces at herself in the spotted mirror that hung above the empty fireplace. She rolled up her hair and coiled it on the top of her head and mocked her reflection. "The Belle of the Ball!" she said, whirling round and letting her hair fall again. She began to dance. "Come on, Matt."

"Don't be an idiot," he said.

She slumped on the wooden bench and twisted round to examine the inscriptions scrawled on the wall behind her. "J. B. LOVES B. D." she read out. "I wonder who they all were. TED'S, TILL THE SPHINX WINKS — well, that was nice for Ted, wasn't it? Before the Housing Estate was built it was all woods and fields round here, Mr. Ricardo told me, and big houses with gardens. People used to come out on the train and go for walks — the animals went in two by two, ages and ages ago." She found another inscription. "UP THE REBELS! I wonder what that was in aid of?"

"None of it matters now anyway," Matt growled crossly. Up the Rebels! It was a battle cry, a call to arms, a desperate voice raised when times were harsh and hard, a revolt against things as they were. Half-heartedly he imagined himself doing a subtle piece of detective work, and restoring a helpless and fragile Madge to the arms of grateful parents. But Madge didn't fit into the picture, and that sort of thing was too much bother — and fairy-book stuff, anyway. "We aren't kids any more — well, are we?" Henry had said. Anyway, Madge didn't care. She was rattling the rusty slot machines, trying to coax a miracle out of them. She gave it up in disgust and moved to the door.

"Rain's over now," she called. "Let's move."

Just as they had reached the door of the waiting room, the train went through at speed. This time they hadn't heard it coming. It seemed to leap from nowhere through the darkness — they felt it pushing the air back against them so that they could hardly breathe. The long column of lighted coaches went past in front of their faces, swaying. There was no time to identify the shapes at the windows as people. Then the last coach and the guard's van cleared them. Now they could see the rails again and the wall on the other side, and the sky. The wheels of the departing train threaded a brisk pattern through the network of points.

Madge blew out a long breath of enjoyment. "I was terrified, weren't you?"

"No," he lied. "Look, it's too early yet for you to go home, what'll you do?"

"Hang around," she said. "I wonder if it's worth waiting here on the chance of another train."

Quickly, so that he wouldn't have time to think better of it, he asked, "Have you ever been back?"

Unlike Henry, she didn't ask, "Back where?" She said no, she hadn't.

The idea grew once Matt had suggested it. He didn't want to sound too keen in case Madge thought it was amusing. She had a habit of being amused. "We could get a bus. Why don't we?"

"What for?" Madge said, and without waiting for an answer went on. "Yes. All right, then. Let's."

As soon as it was settled the horrible question of money cropped up in his mind. He supposed he would have to buy two tickets. He thought he only had enough for one. Furiously he remembered Henry's fat envelope. His own scanty pocket money was due tomorrow; it never lasted round from Saturday to Saturday. Of course he ought to tell Madge right away that he hadn't enough but the idea choked him. Miserably he shinned over the wall after her and stood in silence at the bus stop. She had the sense to stand a little apart from him as if they didn't belong, but this was scant consolation. Now the lights of the bus had appeared, it was drawing in to the curb. He must say something.

"Look —" he began, his voice thick with shame, but Madge turned and pushed a coin into his hand. "The money for the dance," she said. "Here's half. We'll each buy our own fare. A present from Cousin Maudie."

He sat in the seat beside her feeling indignant and grateful and thinking how complicated life had become. It would have been worse if it had been Madge's money. Madge had a job in a supermarket and hated it. The headmaster had been keen for her to stay on at school but Cousin Maudie gave off about it, and said it was time she started earning. She had to grow up, hadn't she, Cousin Maudie said. Madge said she'd hated school as much as she hated the supermarket so it didn't matter anyway.

Sometimes in the months since he had left Dove Square Matt had thought of going back, but he had never gone. Perhaps it was better to remember places than to revisit them. In any case everybody said the Happy Land was so super and how lucky they were, and the gang of children who had fought for St. George had fallen apart after the move. They were living in different blocks of flats — you didn't meet them so often and when you did they looked changed and you felt they noticed a change in you. Things had got a bit polite and posh all round, and you didn't like admitting you'd rather have had them the old way.

The bus had now reached the outskirts of familiar territory. Familiar? Here was the corner beside the Police Station, but no important lamp burned outside it tonight. Now they were rounding the front of the Cinema. How strange it looked! No queues, no names in lights. They came down the steps of the bus and stood on the platform. They passed the place where Mr. Taffe's fish shop used to be, with the gilded fish suspended above the door. At night you couldn't see the wires that supported it, and the street lamp shimmered on the scales so that it seemed to swim through air — but now the air was empty. Ah — that was the high wall beside the Baths, or was it? Matt's mind galloped, chasing landmarks. Mr. Ricardo's restaurant — of course he knew it wasn't there any more, but he couldn't prevent his nose from exploring the air for the fragrance of sizzling chips. And then a final corner and the bus stopped.

"Dove Square," the conductor called.

◄ 3 ►

HE was so sure that they had got off at the wrong stop that he took a step toward the bus again to try to jump on it before it moved, but Madge gripped and held his arm. "It is the right place, Matt. We're here."

Her voice sounded peculiar, as if she too needed to convince herself. The bus went on its way, turned another corner, and was out of sight. There was now no sound at all. This was the first difference in Dove Square. The second difference was that there seemed to be a lot of air about. For a long moment they stood on the pavement just staring. The street lamps showed them everything — and how little there was to see. One wouldn't have minded it all being so different if at the same time parts of it hadn't been so much the same.

The houses of Dove Square were still there, those great solid houses where once long ago the gentry had lived, a house to each family, with their cooks and nurses and housemaids stowed in the basement and the attics, and the family taking up all of the large rooms that lay between. And when the gentry moved out to houses in the new suburbs, Matt and Madge and their friends had lived here, five or six families to a house, sharing the rooms and the stairs and the landings and the taps and the broad front steps, until the City Planning Department had scooped them up and set them down in flats in the Happy Land.

The Dove Square houses hadn't altered. They still had their handsome shabby porches and decorated gateposts, crooked balconies and holes in the wall where the brass doorbells once had been. But the steps were empty now, weeds grew high upon them, no lights shone from the windows. There were no festoons of washing strung along the balconies, some of the windows and doors had been boarded up, and the little front gardens that had formerly been almost bare of grass were jungles of growth, since there were no stampeding children to tread them down.

It was when they turned away from the houses and looked into the center of the Square that cold dismay struck them full in the stomach. Where were the railings, where were the trees and the tangle of grass and bushes that had guarded the Church of St. George Without? Where was the church's solid stonework, its peaked roofs, its tower, their friend the weathercock? There was no sign of trees or grass or bushes, no sign of the church itself. Even the railings had been plucked up. Across an open area of rubble and mud, the houses of Dove Square now looked at each other without much interest. In the middle of this desert squatted a couple of small builders' huts. Bits of broken beams which had been piled haphazardly into a fire still smoked. A bulldozer like a sleeping beast was couched at the far corner where the iron gates once stood guard. A high-lift shovel snoozed beside it.

Madge spoke first. "I didn't think it would be like this." It seemed she minded more about buildings than about relations. Matt was terrified by the idea that she was going to cry, though Madge had never been known to cry in the whole of her history.

"What did you expect it to be like, then?" he said roughly.

"Oh, I don't know. It looks so small — where the church was, I mean. I don't see how it can all have fitted into that space."

Indeed it did seem unlikely that this desolate area had once found room for those giant trees, for the tunnel through the bushes down which they had crept to rally in the cause of St. George, for the aisles, the nave, the committee room with its photograph of the whiskered clergyman. Where all these things had been there was a flattened space of mud and broken stone across which

the wind now moved, sometimes pushing a torn scrap of newspaper in front of it in a bored kind of way, sometimes catching at the smoke from the fire and tying it in knots. Here and there the glazed faces of puddles caught the lamplight.

"I don't know what we came for," Madge said in a choked kind of voice.

"Oh, get lost. You said you wanted to come."

They walked slowly round the four sides of the Square, identifying significant windows and doorways, steps and lampposts. There was a hole in the paving stones where the pillarbox used to stand. This additional loss made their depression deeper — it seemed unreasonable, one expected permanence from pillarboxes. They were consoled a little by the sight of the newspaper and sweet shop a little way down a side street, and went to examine it. Half of the small house had been pulled down, the patterns of wallpaper were exposed, and empty grates were suspended indecently in the open air. But the side with the shopwindow in it was still intact, and surprisingly the glass hadn't been broken. The lamplight shone into the window, lighting up a few curled and yellowed comics, garnished with a sprinkling of dead flies.

Matt studied them. "I suppose they were funny once . . . well, they must have been." But the jokes of two years ago were nothing to laugh at.

He began to agree with Madge that it had been a mistake to come back. It had been a silly idea, his idea — he should have had more wit. What had they expected, anyway? A banner of welcome strung across the road, a red carpet and a brass band? And yet Matt knew that he had expected something. He remembered that famous St. George's Day when the Bishop had taken off his coat and pulled the bell rope in his shirt-sleeves, and he thought that surely some triumphal echo, some vestige of glory would still persist. But there was nothing. Nothing at all. It was a washout.

It was at this moment that they heard the footsteps. They were short and light, they were coming closer. He didn't identify them at once but he was positive that he had heard them before, though in his memory they had been brisker. And then with the footsteps the wind brought him the smell. This, in an amazed and grateful instant, he recognized. It was like the sun coming out. He was almost persuaded that Mr. Ricardo's restaurant still stood in its accustomed place and that he was "FRY-ING TONIGHT."

"Fish and chips!" he breathed to Madge, and her face in the lamplight told him that she already knew.

"Yes, but who —?"

"Shut up!" He kicked her skillfully into silence and they backed a few paces and stood waiting.

The approaching figure had now come into range of the lamplight. They saw the two little dogs on their leads, like tugs in charge of an ocean liner. They saw the light shining on a pair of spectacles, saw the antique belted raincoat, the newspaper parcel slung in the string shopping bag, the bare head which every few seconds, regular as a clock, jerked sideways in the movement they remembered so well.

They came forward. "Shaky!" they cried joyfully. "It's Shaky! Shaky Frick!"

The dogs pulled up short, snuffled suspiciously, and yapped. The man halted. He stood to attention, shoulders back, head still jerking as it had done ever since the day the shell exploded in France, years and years ago. Behind the glasses his eyes peered. Matt thought he recognized fear.

"Advance, Corporal Frick, and be recognized!" he called.

Corporal Frick clicked his heels and saluted. Then his face relaxed and he smiled. "Matthew, the boy Matthew," he breathed. "And the girl Madge. Is it really you?"

"Really, really us!"

Matt was already on his knees on the pavement, allowing the two little dogs (the Duke and Duchess) to renew acquaintance. Their tongues were busy on his face. Further identification was unnecessary.

"Well!" Corporal Frick exclaimed over and over again. "God bless my soul! Strike me pink! Fancy that, well fancy that! I never did, indeed I didn't!" He took a handkerchief from his pocket and blew his nose and then made a business of putting the handkerchief away and said, "Long time no see."

"Oh, it is a long time, Mr. Frick," said Madge, "but we often thought about you."

"Did you? Did you now?" His hand felt for the handkerchief again, then decided against.

"We wondered about you, we tried to find where you were, we looked out for you. But with all those hundreds of flats and people moving out there at different times and all the upset and one thing and another — well, you can imagine what it was like!" But in their heart of hearts they knew they could have looked a little longer and harder.

"A very badly organized exercise if ever there was one," Mr. Frick agreed. "Shocking business altogether, personnel dispersed willy-nilly with no top level coordination."

"It was a mess."

"Inadequate liaison, that was at the root of it. The brass hats never learn. Settled in now, have you?"

"More or less."

"Bit of all right out there, is it?"

"It's not bad," they said without enthusiasm.

"Where did they move you to, Mr. Frick?" Madge asked. "It's funny we never saw you. Which of the Estates are you in?"

Shaky stooped to rub the little dogs comfortably at the backs of their ears. He looked a trifle ill at ease. "Actually, I decided against it."

"What do you mean?"

"Not my kind of life, too cushy by a long chalk. And their Graces —" he nodded in the direction of the dogs — "they were definitely against tabloid living."

"Then you aren't out in one of the Estates?"

"No. No stimulus to personal initiative, nothing to get your teeth into, boy."

"Well — where are you living, then?"

Mr. Frick laid a finger against his nose and looked up and down the pavement before he spoke. Then he said cryptically, "One can't be too careful. Their spies are everywhere."

"Tell us, Mr. Frick. Where did you move to?"

He leaned forward. "Actually, dear boy, I didn't."

"You — what?"

"You don't mean — you can't mean —?"

Mr. Frick smiled and nodded. Indeed he did. Indeed he could.

They looked about them at the desolate buildings. "Not here! But — how?"

"A little improvisation, a little caution, a little camouflage."

"Here? Living here! Show us!"

Mr. Frick surveyed the empty pavements and was satisfied they were empty. "In single file, advance!" He turned and led the way.

He took them past the sweet shop and a short distance down the side street, then turned sharply into the walled alley that ran along the back of the houses that fronted the Square. There was just sufficient moonlight to see. The alley, empty of cats, children, washing, bicycles and dustbins, wore a stricken look. Some of the doors that opened into the yards of the Dove Square houses had been broken off their hinges; others hung crookedly. The alley was overgrown with weeds and

44

brambles. They noticed that Mr. Frick trod delicately, so that these were not trampled or laid flat and no trail was left. They copied him, stepping high. He stopped outside a yard where the door from the alley into the yard was still on its hinges. After a swift scrutiny to left and right he lifted the latch and swung this door open. "Look slippy," he ordered. "Don't dillydally on the way." They went past him into the yard. Nettles closed thickly round their ankles. He shut the door carefully, making no sound with the dropped latch. Moonlight showed a water butt in which the moon floated, and a broken lavatory pan shining whitely from its shed. Shaky took a key from his pocket and unlocked the back door of the house. The key turned easily in the oiled lock. He beckoned them to the threshold. Then: "Wait here," he said.

They waited, remembering that the room beyond them had been Ma Flint's kitchen, smelling of baking and washing, of stew and babies, a famous battleground filled with soapsuds and feet and the steady boom of Ma Flint's voice. Shaky Frick went through the room. They heard his footsteps on a flight of stone steps, descending. A match was struck. Then in the basement window, half sunk below the level of the yard, they saw a dim flicker of light, and Shaky's hand appeared and drew the curtains across so that the light was just a faint glow.

Now he was calling to them. "Come in and lock the door behind you!" They obeyed, and then crossed the kitchen and descended the short flight of steps. In the room at the foot of the steps two candle flames steadied and lengthened. Shaky was waiting for them. "Home Sweet Home!" he said. "Not much of a billet by your standards, I daresay, but Home Sweet Home to me!"

The orderliness and cleanliness of the room in comparison with the wilderness outside was the first thing to come to their notice. There was little furniture: a camp bed with neatly folded blankets, a washstand with water lily patterns on its tiles, a table where the candles stood and which also bore a Primus stove, a couple of cane-backed chairs. On the red tiles of the floor a rag mat. Slippers standing to attention beside the bed waiting for their superior officer. A tin-topped trunk with "Frick. C. T. S." painted on it in white capitals. Two brass shell cases gleaming in the candlelight, flanking the clock on the mantelpiece.

Mr. Frick knelt to put a match to an oil stove. "There!" he said rising. "What do you think of it? Not so dusty, eh?"

The light had now crept to the four walls. Matt could see that these were as crowded as the room was bare. From every side photograph frames jostled, eyes looked out at them. There were the eyes of the lady in a beaded low-necked gown who sat on a sofa and fondled a much younger and slimmer Duke and Duchess upon her lap. Matt didn't need to be told that this lady was Mrs. L'Estrange. Mr. Frick called her his Patroness. He had been her gardener after he came home from the war, wounded and jerking his head, unfit now for his trade as a house painter. At her death he had come into a small legacy with which he was to make a home for the Duke and Duchess. That was why the dogs had such a haughty look, they knew they had money in the bank. Next on the wall to Mrs. L'Estrange was a royal head, large sad eyes and ample moustaches. Matt had a stamp with this King's head on it in his stamp album. The Queen, in a gown whose neck was as high as Mrs. L'Estrange's was low, flanked her spouse's portrait.

Other pictures too. There was a picture of the whiskery clergyman from the Church of St. George Without (The Reverend Robinson Crusoe), several pictures of the Duke and Duchess smirking beside silver cups much larger than they, a group of people in old-fashioned clothes holding flags and crowded together on the steps of one of the houses in Dove Square. "Armistice Day," Corporal explained. And there was a photograph of Corporal Frick himself, erect and in full uniform, holding his head as still and proud as a statue, which showed it had been taken before the shell exploded.

Above the mantelpiece a Union Jack was stretched. Below it was a glass case containing medals.

"Well, what do you think? Snug, eh?" Shaky asked.

"It's wonderful, Mr. Frick," they agreed.

" 'If you knows of a Better 'Ole,' " he said with pride. He pulled out the two chairs and they sat down. He found a box on which to seat himself. "Not really organized to do much entertaining," he explained, "more in the nature of a field station, really. Comfortable enough, are you? Everything hunky-dory?"

47

Very, they said awkwardly, oh, very hunky.

"Now — tell me everything," he commanded. "Begin at the beginning and go right through."

Madge reminded him of his fish supper. "It'll be getting cold," she said.

"So it will, so it will." Mr. Frick took down three plates from the shelf, opened the newspaper, and divided up what was there. Matt by this time was ravenous. He accepted his share gladly, wondering why Madge insisted she wasn't hungry, thank you, and why she emptied what was on her plate back on Shaky's plate, and why she glowered at Matt so fiercely in the candlelight.

"Now — everything!" Mr. Frick said again, and they told him everything, answering his questions about friends from Dove Square, their families, their health, their jobs. "All very high class and stylish out there, so I believe," Shaky said. He fed chips to the Duke and Duchess, who sat up and received them neatly, keeping their lips disdainfully curled. "All very la-di-da, so the little lad told me. Although I don't think he fancied it very much."

"What little lad?"

"One of the pale-haired family that used to live overhead — Flint, the name was. Sammy Flint."

Madge looked alarmed. "Sammy? I know when he was lost last Christmas, they found him here. Does he come back?"

"He used to, until I told him to stay away."

"What did he come for?"

"I think he hadn't quite got it into his head that he

didn't live here any more. A kind of homing instinct, perhaps. Oh, we had some fine talks, young Sammy and I. I miss him."

"Could you understand what he was saying, Mr. Frick?" Matt asked.

"As near as made no matter. But then a gang of rough no-goods came around taking the place apart. Wrecking. Smashing. I heard them at it. Anything that wasn't smashed already, they had to smash it. I thought it was healthier for young Sammy if he stayed away. No place for a child. Don't come back, I told him. Now, what about young Queenie Harrison? You haven't told me about her."

"No, we haven't," they agreed.

"Blooming, is she?"

They were embarrassed. Miss Harrison was another of the old Dove Square friends they hadn't kept up with. It was hard to explain. Nobody was ashamed of knowing Miss Harrison, why should they be? She was a nice old girl. It was just that things were different out at the Happy Land. People seemed to hide behind their own four walls more. What was the good of a front door if you didn't close it? There was no meeting on stairs and landings, no queuing for taps, no spilling over into the street, no calling from backyard to backyard, no sitting out on the front step to watch who went by and swap comics or dry your hair or chew sweets. You were meant to be self-contained — all right, you were self-contained.

And Miss Harrison had somehow dropped out. Probably she was housed in the block which provided small flatlets for elderly people who lived alone. Matt's conscience imagined her sharing her solitude with her sewing machine. He wished Shaky hadn't asked this question, and sucked his final chip until it was rigid and greasy.

"Well, if you do run into young Queenie tell her Charlie Frick sent his regards," Shaky said. "Till Hell Freezes, tell her," and they promised that they would. He boiled a kettle on the Primus and they drank hot tea. The oil stove had made the room warm, the candles in their halos of blue light burned brighter and taller so that the stems became luminous and hot grease poured down them and turned solid. The eyes from the photographs seemed to glow, to smile.

"How do you manage here, Mr. Frick?" Madge asked. "Isn't it lonely?"

"Lonely?" His eyes traveled over the walls.

"And no water and no electricity."

"Candlelight, oil stove, Primus. Rainwater from the butt in the yard for ablutions, and I take my water bottle with me when I go out." He showed them his water bottle, khaki-covered and with leather straps to go over his shoulder. It still bore his regimental number stamped on the side. "I wear it under my British warm," he explained. "A friend who has a garage fills it up for me, strictly on the Q.T. of course — a chap I can rely on, one of the best but no names, no pack drill, eh?"

"And nobody knows you're here?"

"The Brass Hats don't, that's what matters."

"If they knew they'd move you out."

"You've got it in one, boy. So they would."

He chuckled and turned the blue flame on the oil stove a shade higher. How quiet it was — no traffic here now; nothing to bring traffic except the demolition squads, and they would only come in the daytime.

"What do you do in the evenings, Mr. Frick?"

"Tickle the old cat's whisker," he said. "The Marconi set." He showed them the small box with the knob on it and the stiff extended wire. "Listen to this." He adjusted it; now they heard thin metallic music coming through, like grasshoppers in outer space.

"How long will it be before they begin to pull down the houses?" Matt asked.

Mr. Frick said, "Ah, now you're asking. What about another cup?"

Madge said, "No, really, Mr. Frick. We can't stay." Matt tried to get signals through to her that they could, but she wasn't receiving any.

Matt asked the question that needed to be answered before he went home. "Was it terrible when the trees and the church came down?"

"Yes, boy, it was terrible." The way Mr. Frick said it made it impossible for Matt to ask any more, but the answer afforded him a kind of mournful peace.

Talk dwindled after that. Matt's stomach cried out for food and drink — the few chips had only given it ideas. "I suppose we ought to go," he said, getting up.

"Stretched out quite a bit since I saw you," Shaky

said, looking him up and down. Embarrassed now by his size as well as his hunger, Matt insisted that they really must be off.

"Half a mo till I have a reccy," Shaky said. He extinguished the candles and they sat in darkness until he had gone upstairs and through the yard and inspected the alley. "All clear," he reported, and they negotiated the stairs and the nettles and were standing outside the yard gate.

They heard the bolt of the back door slide across. Corporal Frick had gone to ground.

"Why did you have to go and guzzle his chips like that?" Madge asked fiercely as soon as they had moved off down the alley. "You might have known he'd only have enough for one. You are a greedy guts, Matt."

Matt was immediately angry because this hadn't occurred to him. "Well, he offered them, didn't he?"

"And if we'd had more tea, he'd never have had enough milk left for his breakfast. You ought to think."

"How do you know he wouldn't have had enough?"

"I saw," Madge said.

Matt's stomach gnawed; so did his conscience. Madge still had that annoying habit of hitting nails on their heads.

They emerged from the alley and once again were shocked by the desolation in the Square. They should have remembered and been prepared for it. Instead they looked involuntarily for the treetops, and for the weathercock on his tower. "There used to be an owl, do you remember?" Matt said, because it would help if she would talk about this loss, but Madge didn't answer. She was still on about those chips. "Now he'll be hungry, and it's your silly fault."

"He's as crazy as they come. What does he want to stay on there for anyway?" Matt growled. "He's crazier than ever if you ask me, and that's saying something."

"I think he's splendid." Madge's eyes flashed in the lamplight and challenged him.

They snapped at each other all the way back to the bus stop. As the bus approached Matt had another unhappy thought. They would reach the Flats just about the time the cinema and the Youth Club and the protest meeting and the pub and everything else would be getting out. The pavements would be crowded. Everyone would see them getting off the bus together, Madge and him. That wasn't going to be very funny. Some people went around in pairs and nobody said or thought anything. Gwen looked as if she was aiming to beat her big sister's performance for a speedy turnover of boyfriends, and her big sister had held the record in Dove Square. (You saw her sometimes nowadays pushing the twins' pram round the shops.) Henry generally had a girl with him in the evenings, Eddie might have, Sidney sometimes had. Now people would see them together and think he'd made a date with Madge. With Madge! Well, that was one thing they weren't going to think —

The bus drew in to the curb and stopped, panting with impatience. As Madge stepped on he said, "Think

I'll walk it back," and swung on his heel, hungry, miserable and thoroughly cross. The bus moved off with Madge inside.

The rain had ceased some time ago but the Happy Land was a fair distance away, on the city outskirts. He wasn't sure of the route so he set his course by the red lights at the top of the hospital chimney — these stuck out like illuminated raspberries on the city skyline. No matter where you were, you saw them. If he steered by them he couldn't go far wrong. Soon he had reached a main road and was glad of the comfortable sight of lighted shops and the moving traffic. One of the shops had FISH AND CHIPS written up outside it; perhaps this was where Shaky made his purchase. It was too much! Matt's fingers, tightening inside his pocket, closed on money — the change he'd had out of his bus fare.

The possibilities of quieting his conscience and his ravenous stomach struck him simultaneously. He could go in and spend the money — Cousin Maudie's money — and munch his way home. Or — he almost wished he hadn't thought of it — he could go in and spend Cousin Maudie's money and buy a fish supper to take back to Mr. Frick — just a little present, Mr. Frick, while I happened to be passing. Next time he ran into Madge, if he did run into her, he'd enjoy telling her. It would be worth it. He made his mind up quickly and went into the shop.

The parcel was warm and yielding in his hands and smelled abominably tantalizing. He hadn't bought a fish supper for months — people in the Happy Land had got a bit too polite for fish suppers. They took packets of fish fingers home in paper bags and heated them up and ate them off plates, pretending they tasted just as good. The rising smell tickled his nostrils. I'll need to hurry, Matt said to himself, if this is going to reach Shaky. Manfully he swallowed his saliva and at a gallop turned again in the direction of Dove Square, hoping that St. George was on his side. But probably the Saint had an appetite as hearty as his own.

He turned two corners and slowed to a jog trot. He had a stitch in his side and his stomach cried aloud for consideration. The warmth from the fish supper, which he carried clasped against his chest, had reached through to his skin. Come *on*, St. George! He fixed his mind on some of the choicer tortures he'd seen on the telly, on hunger strikers and charity posters for needy people and on the heroism of the early Christian martyrs. If they could do it — ! One chip, his stomach pleaded, just one little crisp golden chip! He tightened his grasp on the parcel and went forward, hammering his feet down hard on the pavement to show himself that he meant it. Not far to go now. He thought of Madge and how agreeable it would be to chizz her.

As the streets became quieter the sound of his footsteps grew more loud. Too loud altogether, something warned him. You can't go stampeding into Shaky's No-Man's-Land like a herd of bullocks. Easy now, easy does it. Caution grew in him and he was walking almost on tiptoe when he turned once more into what was left of Dove Square.

Ten yards off he saw the man and felt the cold breeze of fear. The man had his back to him; he had not heard him coming. He was too much absorbed in what he was doing. What was he doing? He was stooping low, fumbling with spread fingers at the wall. Then he straightened and took something from his pocket. Matt heard the scrape of a match and saw the uncertain flame flicker and disappear. Another match, this time more carefully shielded in the man's cupped hands. He bent down again, holding the little patch of moving light against the wall. Now Matt knew what he was doing. This was where the metal nameplate was fastened, the plate that bore the inscription "DOVE SQUARE." Somebody had been amusing himself with it, so that now the dirty metal only read "OVE QUA " but apparently this was enough. The man blew the match out — he had found what he was looking for. And then, as the man turned his head sharply in his direction, Matt froze and became part of the darkness.

He realized what had happened. The same wind that had blown out the first match had carried the smell of the fish supper across the ten yards of pavement between them. His presence was known. But there was something else. The flame that gave this man his bearings had also shown his face to Matt. It was a face he knew and already disliked. It was the face of the Salesman.

And now he heard the Salesman's voice. "Hallo, there," he said quietly. "Not a bad evening since the rain eased."

Matt stood stock still with his thoughts racing. To be betrayed by a fish supper was just his rotten luck. So much for good intentions, so much for heroism. And now the man was coming toward him. "Just a moment, I'd like a word with you," he said.

Play it cool, Matt told himself. He hasn't really seen you, all he's seen is a patch of darker darkness that is the shape and size of a boy and that smells of fish supper. "I think you might be able to help me," the man said. His voice was pleasant, but behind the pleasantness there was a threat, and he was walking with springing steps that could easily break into a run.

Just as the man's hand shot out Matt ducked and ran. Up one side of the Square and along the next. He ran fast, but the man was gaining on him. Any moment now fingers would close on his shoulder. He'd been a fool to run, but since the chase was on he must keep on running.

He made a quick decision, and on the third side of the Square he put on an extra spurt and slipped down the side street. He knew that he'd gained a few yards — it might be enough. He dodged into the alley that ran at the back of the houses, praying that the man, who had not yet rounded the corner, would run on past. In the blackness of the alley he crouched, fighting back the noise of his own breath.

The man was coming now. His feet thundered past the opening of the alley. Matt felt dizzy with relief. I've done it, I've fooled him. But the footsteps slowed, then stopped. Now they were coming back. They paused inquiringly. The man's bulk made the darkness at the mouth of the alley darker. Then he laughed softly. "So that's where you're hiding, is it?" he said, sniffing. And came forward.

There was nothing else he could do. Matt began to run down the alley. The man must not catch up with him between these narrow walls. This is what a fox feels like, he told himself. And then, suddenly realizing that a fox must carry his scent along with him but that *he* needn't, he dropped the fish supper and sped on unimpeded.

He heard the man's feet skid as they met the parcel, heard him swear, and felt a momentary pang for the golden crispness trodden into dirt and weeds. He forced himself to a quicker pace. The man had been delayed, but only for a few seconds. Now he was coming on again.

This was Shaky's gate; this was the moment of decision. Had he gained sufficient ground to do it? He must take the risk. Silently he lifted the latch. He was through!

Again the man's footsteps slowed, stopped. Matt could hear his heavy panting. Then he heard something that made him sick with fear. The latch of the gate into Shaky's backyard was lifted — the gate swung open, and the latch was eased again into its place. The man was in the yard with him. He was cornered. The few yards between them had shrunk to a few feet.

Astonishingly, the man didn't move at once, and when he did it was not in Matt's direction. Matt was sure the Salesman guessed where he was standing. But the man went past him, almost brushing against him. Like a thread that snaps, the hunt was off.

The man was moving toward the dim shape of Shaky's lighted window. Matt's relief changed to the sharpness of self-reproach. This was Shaky Frick's yard. This was also Shaky Frick's front door. And he had led the man straight to it.

He could have got clear away if he'd wanted to, but because it was his fault he was now determined to stay. The light from the basement half-window was obscured by the man's stooping back. He was peering into the room. There was a slit between the curtains. Suddenly the man straightened up and went forward. The stillness was broken by the sound of knuckles rapping on wood. Absolute silence. Matt saw in his mind's eye the frozen fear on Shaky's face. The knuckles rapped for the second time.

"Come on, you in there," the man said softly. "Open up, Friend Frick!"

The pause that followed was so long that Matt thought it would stretch out for ever. He waited for the man to knock again. But before he did so the bolt slid, the key was turned, and a golden bar of light spread across the nettles as the door was eased open a few inches.

"Who is it? What do you want?"

The man must have laid his weight against the door and forced it back. For a few moments the yard was floodlit. "Well, Friend Frick — and about time!" the

man's voice said. The little dogs lifted their voices from the basement in a muffled uproar. The door was drawn close and secured. Now the man was inside with Shaky.

Matt went through the yard and when he had reached the house he dropped into the little well that surrounded the basement window. He crouched low in the nettles with his head at the level of the sill. Now he could see what was going on in the room.

The Salesman stood with his back to the window, facing Shaky. At each side of him the Duke and Duchess had taken up positions with their lips curled back, swearing at him through their teeth. Shaky stood very straight, but he was holding the edge of the table and his face was small and gray.

"Get out," he was saying. "Get out!"

"Not much of a welcome to an old friend, is it?"

"Did you say friend?"

The man laughed. "Have it your own way."

"I'll do that, don't you worry," Shaky said. "What is it you want?"

"Ah, that's better. Let's sit down and talk it over comfortably, shall we?" The man began to move towards a chair, then looked at the Duke and Duchess and changed his mind. "I want a little bit of information, that's all," he said, "and you can guess what it is. Things have changed in these parts; I hardly knew the place."

"I'm not surprised. You never were what I'd have called a regular visitor, were you?"

The man ignored this. "It's a poor thing when you

come back and find old friends have gone. Everyone been moved out, have they?"

"Yes."

"You'll be moving out yourself one of these days, I daresay."

Shaky didn't answer. There was a long pause, broken only by the steady growling of the little dogs.

"Now look, Friend Frick," the Salesman said, "no use beating around the bush. You never liked me very much, did you? I was never what you'd call really popular around here, except in one quarter. Where did they go, that's what I'm after. You know who I mean. You tell me where they went, I leave you alone. It's as easy as that."

"You get no information out of me." Shaky stood stiff as a rod. Nothing but his head moved.

"Ah, come on, let's have the address, you must know. I've been around myself, but in those new Housing Estates you could chase after someone for weeks and never find them."

"Maybe they aren't in a Housing Estate."

"And maybe they are."

The two men stared at each other, each waiting for the other to speak. Matt, glued to the window, shifted his position. One of his legs was leaping with cramp. The nettles had penetrated to his ankles; the dry smell of them made him want to sneeze. The pane was misted over with his breath. Cautiously he rubbed it with the back of his sleeve. The man spoke again. "Down at the

Council Offices I daresay they'd be interested to have your address, Friend Frick."

Shaky grew grayer but didn't move. "You wouldn't tell them."

"You don't know what I might do. Come on. I'm only asking you where they are."

"I don't know."

"Don't give me that. Anyway, you know which of the Estates they went to. That would be something of a help."

"I don't know anything."

"Pity. Ah well. You might remember." The Salesman stepped towards the door with a dog trained on each of his ankles. "I'll call again in a week or so." He paused and looked round. "Nice place you've got here. Snug. Suits your pet dragons. It isn't every place they're keen on animals. Easy on the pocket, too. Pity if you had to leave."

He turned the handle and came out. Matt had only time to duck lower into the nettles. He felt the air stir as the man went through the yard. The yard gate opened and closed again. The man's footsteps went down the alley. Matt knew by the change in sound that he had reached the street. The steps grew fainter. Now they had gone.

The key in Shaky's door was turned, the bolt slid over. The slice of light between the curtains disappeared. Shaky had made his privacy complete.

What should he do now? Matt itched to bang on the

door, tell Shaky what he knew, swear tremendous vows of loyalty, demand a badge to wear, a cause and a battle cry. Remember the Battle of St. George Without, Shaky? We'll rally the gang to your standard like we did then. We'll stand up and be counted. We'll see that the dust is properly bitten by the proper people.

But it wouldn't work, he knew it wouldn't work. In any case this was a private affair that he didn't understand and something inside him prickled with a sense of distress and danger. He needed to think.

Across the city the great bell of the University announced that it was ten o'clock. Each stroke was steady and orderly, waiting till the one that came before had finished speaking. Matt remembered that he was hungry and that he had a long way to go.

Emerging at last from a warren of streets into the open area where the Flats were, he was streaking home when he thought of his errand with Mr. Flint. Then he remembered the news that Madge had so casually given him. Ma Flint had walked out. Madge might as well have been relaying a weather forecast, the way she'd said it. He would have to pass the news on to his mother. This could be tricky. I didn't ask Mr. Flint to come and fix the washer. Why not? He wouldn't be able to, Mrs. Flint has walked out. (He could see his mother's face tighten like it did when anything private and sad, anything that was not really her business came her way.) Has she? How do you know? Probably it's only gossip, you shouldn't listen to gossip, Matt. No, it isn't gossip, Madge told me. Oh — were you talking to Madge? And

64

then more explaining. I see, his mother would say, I see, and close her mouth tight in the way that meant Over and Out.

So he decided that to avoid all this he would call at the Flints' flat before he went home and state his request. Let them do any explaining that was necessary, Madge needn't come into it.

He went up in the lift and knocked at the Flints' front door. From inside came the sound of a junior Flint crying. No one seemed to be doing anything about it. It went on crying. He knocked again. At last the door opened a few inches. One eye and a tuft of pale hair appeared. One of the twins, Matt thought, judging from the distance between the hair and the floor.

"Who is it?"

"It's me — Matt."

"You can't come in."

"I don't want to come in."

"What do you want?"

"I've got a message from my mum."

"What is it?"

"It's for Mr. Flint."

"Pa's busy."

"Will you give him the message? It's about our washer. Mum wants him to come and fix it."

"She ought to tell the caretaker."

"She has, he hasn't done anything. Mr. Flint came before when it was the cooker."

"Pa's not doing any evening jobs."

The bunch of hair and the eye were withdrawn

smartly and the door was shut. Well, that was that. Whoever was doing the crying was still at it. Matt heard it all the way down the stairs.

I called at Mr. Flint's and he's not taking on any evening jobs. I don't know, they didn't say. That was what he would tell his mother. The idea gave him little comfort. Unhappiness seemed to be catching. Come *on*, St. George. But there were kinds of unhappiness for which a war cry and a gathering of the clans were no earthly use.

4

THE idea that something must be done nagged at Matt right through Saturday. He woke with it and it was still there when he went to bed. He sucked at the idea as if it was a sweet, but unlike a sweet it grew bigger instead of smaller. It was bigger still on Sunday morning. On Sunday afternoon it was very big indeed.

"Mooching about in the house," his mother said. "Why don't you find something to do?"

His imagination was having a field day. He imagined Shaky and the little dogs, destitute and homeless, roaming the streets — all his silly fault. He imagined the sinister Salesman squeezing the information he wanted out of Shaky — he would know how to squeeze — and appearing on the doorstep of his old friends from Dove Square. Who were they, these friends? And why was he so keen to find them anyway? Matt couldn't imagine anyone being glad to see that unpleasant piece of work on their doorstep. But then he couldn't really imagine Shaky betraying them, whoever they were, so he was back where he started — Shaky and the little dogs, destitute and homeless, roaming the streets. His silly fault. It didn't get any better no matter which way you looked at it.

It was too big to keep it to himself. He had to tell someone, so in the end he decided on Henry. He didn't suppose this would be much help — Henry wasn't what you'd call a Master Brain in spite of his pay packet — but at least he would be a pair of ears, and that was what Matt needed.

He found the pair of ears — gosh, Henry hadn't half let himself loose over his sideburns! — cocked outside the Disc Bar beside the cigarette booth. Oh, very smooth Henry looked in that corduroy jacket and the flower-patterned shirt. You knew by the way he was listening very hard to the record playing inside the shop that he wasn't really listening. The record was just giving him something to do while he waited for whatever it was he was pretending he wasn't waiting for.

"Hiya!" Matt said.

"Hail yourself!" Henry replied in an offhand kind of way, keeping time to the tune with his head as if he was one of the panel on Juke Box Jury and would have to deliver a verdict on it as soon as it stopped.

"Oh, come off it," Matt said. "It won't make the charts, that one." Henry didn't answer, just let loose a kind of inward smile, so Matt said, "I say, did you see Gwen just now? Climbing on the back of a motorbike round the corner?"

Henry lost count of the beats in the bar and said why should he have seen her anyway, and Matt said it wasn't a bad bike, plenty of speed there, and that Gwen was wearing her eyelids green this time.

Henry said did Gwen say anything and Matt said she

said hallo, that was all, and Henry said whose bike was it, and Matt said it wasn't anybody he knew but he looked a groovy type. Henry sagged a bit and said so what and Matt said so nothing, except that the last time he'd seen Gwen she'd had blue eyelids and he thought he liked the green ones better. And Henry said he'd better tell her so, she might be interested, and Matt said he might do just that. And then, because Henry looked thoroughly softened up, he said, "Listen, Henry, I want to talk."

Henry said did he have to and Matt said yes, and Henry said all right then, where? And Matt said, "What's wrong with here?" because anywhere else might involve cash, and he didn't want to fall for any more of Henry's charity doughnuts. Even doughnuts would be wasted on someone who was feeling as guilty as he was.

"It's private business," he decided. "Maybe we'd better go where we're sure we won't meet anyone." So they walked across the grass in front of the Flats to where the big piece of modern sculpture was parked — a pair of lopsided binoculars with ears attached — and Matt told Henry all about it, ending with "If it hadn't been for me nobody'd have found out where Shaky was living."

"O clot of clots!" Henry said helpfully. "O foolish and unwise generation!" And Matt said yes he knew about that but what were they going to do, and Henry said wait a minute who did he think he meant by "they" and Matt said oh, anybody, and Henry said that was all right then, so long as it wasn't him.

"Look, Henry," Matt said. "I'm not asking you to do anything, but what would you do? If it had happened to you, I mean."

"To begin with I wouldn't be such a bird brain as to take a fish supper with me when I went sleuthing, if you really want to know. I'll bet you didn't half stink!"

"I didn't take it with me, I just had it. Anyway I was going to hand it over to Shaky Frick."

"I always said that character was loony. Mad as a hatter," Henry remarked. "Why can't he be like other people and move out? What's wrong with the Flats anyway?"

This was beside the point and Matt didn't want to start on it. "It isn't only Shaky I'm bothered about," he said. "It's whoever it is that the Sinister Salesman is trying to get in touch with."

"You can't be sure he's all that Sinister. For all you know he's their rich uncle from Australia come home rotten with what it takes."

"He isn't anybody's rich uncle from anywhere," Matt snapped. "You've only got to look at him to know that."

Henry licked his forefinger and smoothed down his sideburns thoughtfully, one and then the other. "Look Matt, you're too big a boy now to play Cops and Robbers. Why don't you be your age?"

"If you could see Shaky," Matt fumed, knowing his face had burst out scarlet like a kid's face in the middle of measles. "If you could just see him! He's little and old and — valiant. And he's scared — scared right through to his guts. If you came and saw him —"

He stared at the lopsided binoculars, waiting for Henry to laugh. Surprisingly, Henry didn't.

"Well, why not?" he said. "Let's go and see him then. 'Lead on, Macduff,' as Willy the Sheik used to say when I was a lad at school."

A bus came along as if it had been expecting them, and they got on. Matt felt so grateful to Henry for agreeing to come that he broke into next week's pocket money to pay both fares.

He hoped things were going to work out all right. Surely when Henry had seen Shaky he wouldn't be able to help worrying about what might happen to him, and with two of them worrying it would be more bearable. Already he felt a little better for having told Henry what an idiot he had been.

Henry, however, seemed to be feeling worse. Any enthusiasm he had shown had melted away. It had been a mistake to choose to sit on the top of the bus and in the front seat. The afternoon was fine and the streets were full of lordly motorbikes carrying girls with eyelids of every shade behind their riders. Henry sat slumped in gloom, pretending he didn't see them. But sun in late November shone so rarely that it made a festival of the Sunday parade, and Henry on the top of the bus had a grandstand view.

"I don't know what I came for, I'm sure I don't," he groused. "You do have some weird ideas, Matt. And I'll tell you this, if you've got any bows of burning gold stuffed up your jersey you can leave them there." The bus was held up by a lorry, and a couple of bikes tucked their elbows in and streaked past with powerful grace. Henry groaned. Matt's spirits sank even lower and they had touched rock bottom before the bus arrived at Dove Square.

There was still hope that when Henry saw the desolation in Dove Square he would be impressed. At the moment Henry's glasses didn't betray a gleam — they might have been made of lead. But if Henry could get worked up into one of his fine Old Testament rages about the way things were, then his spectacles would light up and banners might yet be raised. Henry was like that. Once he minded about anything —

By now they were on home ground. "That's where Mr. Taffe's fish shop used to be," Matt said. "I wonder what they did with the outsize goldfish that hung outside. And the Police Station — do you remember the lamp?" But the loss of these things raised not even a flicker of interest from Henry. The bus drew up at the stop and they got out.

"Well," Matt said when Henry had had a chance to look about him, "here we are. What do you think?"

Hopefully he waited for Henry's indignation, but Henry just gazed around unmoved and said, "O abomination of desolations, it's a right old dump, isn't it?"

"I told you it was changed."

"I'll say it is. It never was much of a select neighborhood, I suppose, but I didn't think it was as crummy as all this. What do we do now?"

"We'll take a look around if you like," Matt said, feeling wretched. He went on ahead, leaving Henry to follow or not as he chose. It hadn't worked after all. Henry wasn't staggered, not even impressed, he'd been a fool to hope that he would be. The truth was that Henry had taken to life in the Happy Land from the word go. The Flats suited him. He liked things to be streamlined and plastic-topped and numbered and tailored specially for him. He felt no kind of affection for the faces of the old stone houses, blind-eyed in the brilliant sunlight, the way Matt did. The wasteland where the church had been was any old wasteland. The wind was welcome to move unhindered across the space where once the tower had stood solid. In any part of the city where demolition squads were at work you saw private color schemes exposed to the passerby and bedroom grates hanging in the open air like baskets. There was nothing tragic about it, or indecent.

Matt had gone down one side of the Square and was starting on the next side when he realized Henry wasn't close behind. "Come on," he called without looking back. "Come on if you're coming."

But Henry wasn't coming. He was standing halfway along the first side of the Square, apparently rooted to the pavement. Even when Matt yelled at him again he didn't stir, only stood glaring at the ground.

Matt had to turn and go back for him. Henry didn't look up till he came alongside. "Look," Matt said, "have you gone deaf or something? I've been shouting." And then he saw the glitter in Henry's spectacles and hope rekindled.

"They've moved it," Henry said. "They've taken it

away. Just come and yanked it up, that's what they've done! Of all the rotten — lousy — stinking —" But words were no help to him, and he dried up.

"I don't know what you're on about," Matt said, and then he looked at the pavement when Henry was looking and he did know.

"It was always here! Always!" Henry said. And now there was nothing to be seen except the round hole in the paving stones where the pillarbox had stood.

So the loss of the pillarbox had struck Henry a grievous blow too. With so many other things to mourn over this was an odd thing to pick on but Matt didn't try to work it out, he was content to be grateful. Now they might be getting somewhere.

Henry had begun talking again. "I mean someone might want to post an important letter, you never know, people do post letters," he said. "And you expect to find a pillarbox where you left it. If pillarboxes start moving around — well, I ask you!" He raised eyes to heaven. "Some things just shouldn't be allowed," he fumed. "There is a limit." Twenty years from now Henry would write very successful letters to the papers stating just what the limit was and signing himself "A Rate Payer" or "Pater Familias." But now he was just plain furious.

"We used to wait for the postman to come round and unlock the door and take the letters out of the wire cage, remember?" Henry said. "And wonder who they were from and what they said and if he'd remember to change the little ticket that said when the next collection was.

And when it came to Christmas it was choking full of letters, they were spilling out through the slot. And when the snow came you could measure how many inches by the hat on the top." He went on and on. Matt didn't suppose Henry had ever posted a letter at the pillarbox except perhaps his auntie's Pools coupon, but it made no difference to his sense of loss.

When at last he showed signs of easing off Matt said, "Well, what about going and paying Shaky a call, it's what we came for," but Henry with a look of contempt said, "Not in full daylight, clot! Anyway, let's take a look round first and see what else they've been and done to the old place." And Matt, realizing that he'd made another strategic mistake but that it had been a useful one, allowed Henry to lead the way.

The trouble with Henry had always been that he was harder to stop than to start. When he did things he didn't do them by halves, he gobbled them up whole and entire and looked around for more. And now that the changes in Dove Square had affected him, a whole Conference of Minor Prophets couldn't have radiated such black indignation.

Matt followed close behind as Henry stalked round the Square wailing and lamenting. If he'd had an old shirt on instead of the flower-sprinkled one, he would have rent it there and then. If there'd been any ashes handy . . . he mourned the weathercock, the owl, the Dragon cat, the railings that guarded the secret tunnel, the trees within the railings, the machine at the corner that used to dispense candy, the faces of the stone angels in the church, the picture of St. George set into the floor, the giant ice cream cornet in the window of Mr. Ricardo's shop, the FRYING TONIGHT sign in liquid red writing that wrote itself and then disappeared and began to write all over again on top of its own ghost that still remained at the back of the onlooker's dazzled eyes. Here was the wall at the warehouse side of the Square, against which the boys played games of skill with a ball; here was the tallest of the lampposts, round which the girls bound a looped rope and then sat in the loop while the untwisting rope swung them round and round; here was the best pitch for marbles, the smoothest run for roller skates. Henry remembered them all. He blamed the things that had gone for their absence and sorrowed over the things that were still there because they were still there. He accused the things that were the same of being unchanged and the things that were changed of being different. He called down universal woe on the heads of the city planners as he walked round the four sides of the Square. "Of a truth," he said, "many houses shall be desolate, even great and fair, without in-habitant."

On the door of each house a notice had been nailed: ANY PERSON SEEN DAMAGING THIS PROPERTY IS LIABLE TO PROSECUTION. Judging from the glass-strewn steps, the boarded doors and windows, the basement areas filled deep with rubbish, the wrenched balconies, the missing downspouts, the daubed walls, either the local magistrates must be working nonstop or else the police in the locality were as blind as bats.

"Houses shouldn't be left to rot away like this!" Henry fumed. "Why didn't they make a proper job of it while they were at it? What was wrong with just blowing the whole lot up?"

One of the gateposts with the round stone ball that had decorated the top had been pushed over — the round stone ball lay cracked on the ground. Henry stirred it with the toe of his shoe and it fell apart, like a miniature world disintegrating. "We used to draw faces and stick hats on them, remember?" He looked up the steps. "There is where we lived," he said with a peculiar tone in his voice. "First floor front we were. Coming in, are you?"

The house was a few houses distant from the one where Shaky had dug himself in. Even if someone saw them and came after them there was no reason why Shaky's hideout should be betrayed.

Matt asked, "How are you proposing to get inside? Do we just ring the bell?"

"I know how to get into my own house, thank you very much," Henry snarled, and preceded Matt up the steps, walking in the stiff jerky way a dog does when he has reached the point of no return but can't quite explode into action.

It was just chance of course that whoever had boarded the front door up hadn't done the job very well, or perhaps some visitor had been trying his luck with it since. A couple of the boards loosened when Henry wiggled at them. He wiggled some more and they came clean away. "Welcome to my humble abode, sorry it's the maid's day out," he said, stepping sideways through the gap. Matt followed.

It had been dreary enough looking at the houses from the outside, but inside it was so unexpectedly worse as to be almost terrifying. It robbed them of breath and voices. Henry dried up completely. There wasn't another syllable out of him. He'd rather enjoyed putting on a bit of an act out there on the pavement, ranting about in highflown language, blowing things up a bit bigger than they were — partly because he knew Matt was impressed, partly because he enjoyed the sound of his own voice and in his days in the Cathedral Choir he had modeled himself closely on the Bishop.

Now he couldn't utter a word and he knew Matt felt the same. Neither of them had expected that the shabbiness would matter so much. They hadn't known that it would hurt like this. They were ashamed of it and ashamed of themselves because they minded. They'd had some good times here in Dove Square. It had been their place — they had been happy. The desolation and the dirt were insults.

It was no wonder that the walls in the Flats felt so close together. Even the tiled hall here was as broad as a field. The ceiling stretched high above their heads — it was almost obscured by shadows and the webs of innumerable spiders. Matt, staring at the floor, remembered the pattern on the tiles — it had been the same pattern in the hall of the house, two houses farther along, where he and his mother had lived. Once he'd known it by heart. Not that much of the pattern was visible now. What wasn't thick in dust and fallen plaster was covered with splinters of glass from the fanlight, and with the wreckage of the light fitting which some over-energetic visitor had wrenched out of its socket. Wallpaper, torn off in ribbons, lay underfoot like jungle grasses. The air was stale; it had been there a long time.

The lack of furnishings in the hall wasn't so disturbing as the sight of the few items that had been left behind. On the wall at the corner a coat that had grown tired of waiting drooped on its peg, the shoulders grayed over with dust. The umbrella stand of mottled bamboo held a child's paper whirligig and a stick for poking when the gutter got stopped. One Wellington boot lay here — someone must have got into trouble over that. This was the floor where Mr. and Mrs. Lumba and their family used to live, and Wellington boots were required in every size, largest down to smallest. And who had abandoned a saucepan at the foot of the stairs at the moment of flight? What bird had escaped from the open birdcage?

"We'll go upstairs," Henry decided. Across the lowest step lay a banister which had been wrenched out of its position. Henry lifted it and carried it up with him, swinging it as if he was testing its quality.

He opened the door of his aunt's kitchen. Miss Mickle, when she moved to the Happy Land, had left behind her an oil stove, a cooler with the lid ripped off it, and a mangle. The cupboard doors lay open, hanging unevenly from broken hinges. Surprisingly, a colored calendar still sat primly in its place in the center of the mantelshelf, torn off at the month when the exodus had taken place.

"Gosh!" Henry said. "There's something I've just remembered." He went over to the cupboard and took out a drawer. Then he put his hand into the space behind. His glasses gleamed. "They're still here, what do you know!" He withdrew his hand and held it extended. On his palm lay half a dozen marbles. "See those!" he said as if he'd picked up gold nuggets. He put the marbles into his mouth to clean them, then spat and held them out once more, admiringly. "They all had names, but I've forgotten them." He pondered for a while — it was very important to remember the names of the marbles. It was no use, he couldn't. "One of them was Dove Square High Champion, King Over a Hundred," he said, "but I'm not sure now which it was." He looked embarrassed and angry.

He chose the largest of the marbles, and taking careful aim he potted it through the broken pane of the window. Matt watched in silence. It was the obvious thing for Henry to do. The next marble missed the hole and smashed the pane below. With the remaining four marbles Henry succeeded in smashing all the other panes. They could hear glass and marbles rattling down on the roof of what used to be Mrs. Lumba's scullery.

To Matt this noise was like a starting gun. Now the band was playing and all the lights had gone on. Why don't you get something to do? That was what his mother had said. All right, now he had something to do. He set about doing it. His first requirement was a weapon. He selected a banister that fitted his hand perfectly. One determined yank and it came free. Whoever had fitted these banisters in their places years and years ago when Dove Square was built would have been surprised how easy it was to lever them out, one by one, as Matt did now, until they lay at the foot of the stairs like a pile of crazy cricket stumps.

They stormed up to the floor above. This was where Cousin Maudie and Madge had lived. Joyfully they discovered a mattress lying on the floor in one of the bedrooms. They hauled it out onto the landing. "Hallelujah and how! I've got my knife!" The fistfuls of torn-out stuffing, dropping down the stairwell, were impressive. The pillow they found was even better. Henry slit its throat and held it over the banister rail, shaking it from the corners. The feathers took as long as snowflakes do to decide where they would choose to settle. Quite a number came back and chose the shoulders of Henry's corduroy jacket, so that he seemed to be wearing a feather boa.

On the landing Matt saw the small squares of blue and red glass at the corners of the big window. The landing window in his own house had also had these colored panes. He used to look through them at the trees in the Square and the top of the church tower, first in romantic shades of blue, then in fiery red. These colored squares were still unbroken. Since there were no trees and no church outside any more, only a muddy wilderness, it seemed a good reason for gouging out the red and blue glass with the poker which Cousin

Maudie had decided she wouldn't need in the Happy Land. The tough panes of glass didn't yield readily to gouging. In the end he charged each of them singly, stabbing the poker through in a cascade of colored splinters. Each window as he cleared it became a frame for the desolation outside in the Square. The mattress was still occupying Henry; he jabbed his knife into it, splitting and tearing; he uttered strange cries, tore out the stuffing, and scattered white handfuls of it into the stairwell.

At last there didn't seem anything left to do that was really worth the exertion. Whatever it was that they had been doing and for whatever reason, it was done now, was finished. It had grown darker and colder. There was a forsaken feeling in the house, as there is when music ceases and echoes return. By unspoken consent they came down into the hall. Henry picked up a banister from the pile of banisters and aimed it at the umbrella stand, but missed. Instead it struck a couple of milk bottles. One of them was shattered; the other fell over on its side and spun like a wheel. The umbrella stand jeered at them. Matt threw the poker and hit it. It heeled over slowly and took its time to collapse, like a sick animal.

Henry said, "Your hand's bleeding."

Matt sucked it and spat out the salty blood. He was out of breath and very tired. He avoided looking at Henry. He said, "Well, that's that then, isn't it?" He wasn't sure what it had been about or why it had been so important or who the enemy was or if there had been

an enemy. At least it had been done. In a way it had been a funeral. A funeral was necessary. But you were glad when it was over.

"Come on then, if you're coming." He stooped to go through the gap they had made in the door and then heard footsteps on the pavement and pulled up short. "Hang on a minute!"

"Police, is it?" Henry's voice was sharp with fear.

But Matt had recognised the footsteps. "No, not police." They crouched in the gap, watching the street. Shaky and his little dogs went past proudly and privately. Just as he drew level with the boys the street-lamps blinked on and the light shone full on him. Corporal Frick's campaigns were with real enemies. The squad turned the corner, making for the entry at the backs of the houses.

"No point now in going to see him." Henry was stating a fact, not asking for an opinion. Matt had no opinion to offer; he was feeling terrible; he wasn't sure whether he would have to be sick. He went to the back of the hall trying to make his mind up. When his head cleared and he found the sickness was passing, he came back. He wasn't surprised to find that the hall was now empty. Henry had chosen to go on by himself.

Matt had no wish to catch up on him, so he went back up the stairs, past Henry's floor to the floor where Madge and her weird Cousin Maudie used to live. He would wait here a while, give Henry time. The door of the room that had been the kitchen was closed; Henry and he hadn't visited this room. He opened the door and went in. Soft as milk or primroses, the light from the streetlamps shone through the windows and filled the room from wall to wall.

Matt remembered these walls. Cousin Maudie's taste in wallpaper had been as enthusiastic as her taste in new clothes and nail varnish and rinses. The lamplight showed him the huge parakeets still shrieking at each other from their roosts on blue cauliflowers, the galleons battling through purple oceans, the castles raising their tormented turrets into vermilion skies. Here they all were, brilliant and outrageous as ever though no one saw them now. The rectangle of undecorated wall marked the position of the cooker. Cousin Maudie had a taste for hot jazzy music, and rumbaed while she cooked. Ash from her long cigarette holder enriched the stew.

Matt looked for the linoleum daffodils, stirring the dusty floor with his shoe. There they were, tied in bunches of ribbon as Madge had described them. All the kitchens in the Happy Land had identical nonslip easi-clean surfaces. No one had needed to take their lino with them when they left Dove Square and Cousin Maudie's daffodils wasted their fragrance on the desert air. But in the corner nearest the window — surely there was something odd there. He went across the room to find out what it was.

Here the lino had been rolled back, the newspaper that had lain below it was crumpled into a ball and thrown aside, and a floorboard had been wrenched up and stood erect like a solitary tombstone.

Matt knelt and put his hand down between the joists,

feeling to left and right, but there was nothing there, and his fingers met only the ridges of plaster rising from the lathes. The tomb, if it had held anything, was empty.

He came downstairs puzzled. His hand had begun to ache and it was bleeding again. He was bone tired, he was hungry, he was ready for home.

There was no danger now of overtaking Henry — he would be halfway back by this time. Matt took a look out into the street. It was clear. He crawled through the broken door, put the boards back into their place, brushed feathers and dust and plaster from his clothes, stood erect filling his lungs with clean night air, and set off at a determined jog trot for the Happy Land.

⚘ 5 ⚘

GWEN'S green Sunday eyelids, though they had made an impression on Matt, hadn't had any success in the direction they'd been aimed at. She didn't even know whether Ivor (he was the curator of the monster on wheels) had noticed them; he hadn't said anything. But neither had he said anything about her trouser suit (it was the first time she had worn it) or her table tennis earrings, or — come to that — about Gwen herself. While they were traveling along at incredible speeds between cliff-high lorries, or fuming noisily at pedestrian crossings, or leaping forward unleashed when the lights changed, conversation was impossible, and she was much too frightened to talk or to listen. She'd always heard speed did things to you; now she knew.

They stopped for some coffee and at last Ivor was sitting facing in her direction and except for the jukebox it was quiet. He wasn't going to be one of the tongue-tied ones, was he? No, he was leaning forward, anxious to talk. Gwen set her ears in a listening position and fluttered her eyelids in anticipation. Go on, Ivor. I'm listening. He went on. He went on about the bike through three cups of coffee, extolling its looks and its performance, its mood and temper, the way it had been improved by the cunning adjustments he'd done on it; he took it apart and lauded each separate item, and then put them together again, and lo, they fitted. Gwen by this time could only think of the long miles back through the November evening, with the dark ribbons of the hedges pouring over her shoulders and the cats' eyes on the road appearing as one perpetual leer. To cheer herself up she tried to decide which of the dreamy doctors in Casualty she would like to find at her bedside when she woke up in hospital after the accident.

She realised that this misery was all her own fault. She shouldn't have gone with Ivor at all, it was a judgment on her. This had been her Sunday for Youth Club Discussion Group, and her conscience was niggling. By this time she should have been committed knee-deep to a Cause. Outside the hospital Gwen's time was divided between Causes and boys. You colored your eyelids and dressed up for boys, and you wore a clean scrubbed face and casuals for Causes.

Boys on the whole were a disappointment. They were so young; most of them you remembered as kids and when you met them again they seemed to be pretending. Gwen preferred craggy men, the sort you saw advertising shoes and overcoats and whiskey, but you never met them. She had first come across Ivor at the Sports Club and had hopes he might turn out to be craggy, but he hadn't. She decided he was barely adult. Probably he still had a few toy cars stowed away in the corners of his pockets. It had been interesting to Gwen to discover how collectable boys were, but discouraging to learn that they were still boys, and she would be thirty and middle-aged, she supposed, before any of this little lot had turned craggy. Grateful as she was to have reached home safely on that Sunday evening after her trip with Ivor, she wiped off her green eyelids with a sense of disappointment.

This was now Friday and she had decided to make things right with her conscience by going to the protest meeting instead of the weekly Youth Club Dance. But before she came off duty at the hospital the men brought in the stretcher out of the ambulance, and when she had seen who was on it she knew that she would miss this evening's protest meeting as well as the dance, and that someone must be told, right away.

The question was who to tell, and she debated this all the way back to the Happy Land, feeling the little thrill of importance that she used to feel when she was a kid and knew something that nobody else knew. Her mum was working late, so that was no good. There was her big sister who was married now, but she didn't think her big sister was the person to tell this news to. You couldn't really tell her big sister anything these days, she was deaf to all noises except those that came from the twins. Who else was there? Henry? No, Henry would think she'd singled him out for a special favor and she didn't want that. Madge? Perhaps. But you never knew with Madge. Someone, however, must be told.

And then, as she turned up the final stretch of road to

the Flats, Matt dropped without any warning from the high wall beside the railway and landed a few feet ahead of her on the pavement. She accepted him gratefully.

"Hi! Matt!"

Matt turned round. He seemed cross and not at all pleased to see her. Anyway he looked a bit silly, still in a school blazer with a bag full of books and that cap sitting like half a shrunk orange skin on the top of his head.

"Here — Matt — wait for me! I've got something to tell you, it's important!"

"I'm in a hurry!"

It was interesting to meet a boy who was in a hurry in the opposite direction. "Anyway, what have you been doing, coming over the wall like that?" she asked. "Ooh, you don't half look guilty, Matt!"

Matt slowed enough for her to catch up with him, but she still had to trot a little to keep level because he took such very long strides.

"Well, what is it?" he asked sideways.

"I can't run and talk," she panted. "It's all very well for a great big man like you, Matt McGinley, but it's not so easy for a little girl like me."

Under the next streetlamp he stopped and said, "All right then, I'm listening, but make it snappy. And I wish you wouldn't do that."

"Do what?"

"Wiggling your eyelids."

"Oh sorry — was I?"

Matt said yes she was and what was all the fuss about anyway? In her nurse's cap and Burberry and with civilian eyelids and her face a bit tired and shiny, Gwen didn't look any different from some of the girls at school.

"Who do you think I saw being carried in on a stretcher just as I was coming out of Casualty tonight?"

"One of the Monkees," Matt guessed. "It's too early for Father Christmas, I suppose."

Gwen said all right if he wasn't interested she wouldn't tell him, she just thought someone ought to be told, that was all. Matt said how could he tell whether he was interested if he didn't know who it was so couldn't she get a move on, and Gwen said all right then (she gulped the way she always gulped when she was a kid and had something dramatic to say), it was Pa Flint, that's who it was, and he was unconscious by the look of him, and then Matt grabbed hold of her arm so hard that it hurt and said, *"Who?"*

"I told you, Pa Flint. An accident in the street, I heard the man say."

"Gosh!" Matt's face grew very serious. "We'll have to *do* something, Gwen," and he looked at her in a new way that made her toes open and shut a little until she reminded herself that this was an evening for a Cause and she'd got one. She steadied her eyelids and said, "What *are* we to do?"

"She hasn't come back yet, has she — Ma Flint?"

"No. Perhaps she won't, this time."

"She always comes back. You know she does."

"Yes, but when? And what happens in the meantime?"

"That's it," Matt said. "What does happen?"

"I suppose it'll be the Cruelty people," Gwen said, "once they hear about it. Generally they send them to a Home. Sometimes it's to different Homes. If they're in need of care and protection."

"And do you suppose they are?" The Flint family always operated as a tribe and other people needed protection from them.

"The Cruelty people would think so."

"Nobody could split up the Flints."

"They could."

Matt thought for a while. Then he asked, "How would the Cruelty people know about it?"

"The neighbors, or the Almoner at the hospital once she hears about it."

"And who tells the Almoner?"

"You are a nit, Matt — Pa Flint does, of course!"

In the lamplight she saw Matt's face change and take on a look of triumph. "He doesn't tell anybody anything while he's flat out on a stretcher, and none of the neighbors know yet," he said, and Gwen breathed, "Oh Matt, you are wonderful, I knew you'd think of something!" and forgot all about her eyelids.

Luckily Matt didn't notice, and soon they had arranged that Gwen should nip back to hospital and see if she could get a message through to Pa Flint as soon he came round, telling him not to breathe a word to anybody, and that it was all being arranged by friends. Meanwhile Matt would get hold of Madge and when Gwen came back they would meet outside the Flats and decide what ought to be done and who was to do it.

It was only after he'd watched Gwen scudding off to the bus stop, smug and busy and no end pleased with herself, that Matt realized just what he'd let himself in for. Perhaps his plan hadn't been such a bright one after all. Get hold of Madge, Gwen had said. You never noticed girls organizing until they'd done it. Tell Madge what's happened, Gwen had said. Meet you later and we'll talk about what else is to be done, she'd said. And he'd said yes, yes, yes, Florence Nightingale ma'am, whatever you say, Joan of Arc, it's all right, Lady Macbeth, you can leave the daggers safely with me.

In the Dove Square days, telling Madge would have been easy — if she wasn't out on the steps with her hair spread over the railings drying, she'd have been skipping on the pavement with Gwen or scrapping with someone else. You just yelled for her and if you didn't see her you chucked a clod of earth at her window and waited. But in the Flats you went up in a lift and rang a bell and waited politely on the mat until Madge came. Only this was Friday and Madge wouldn't come to the door, he knew that. Friday was the night of the dance at the Youth Club.

Earlier in the evening he'd remembered this was Friday, and he'd gone over the wall to see if she was mooching about in the railway cutting like she'd been the Friday before. Shaky Frick was still on his mind and he wanted to find out whether Madge had had any bright ideas about going to visit him again, though he wasn't going to tell her about Shaky's unpleasant visitor. There was no sense spreading that around too much. But there was no sign of Madge either under the arch or on the platform. He pushed open the door of the waiting room but nothing in the dusty interior moved except his reflection in the mirror. This movement startled him; he'd forgotten the mirror was there. And then he saw that there were letters scrawled in lipstick on the glass. Certainly they hadn't been there before. He went to examine them.

There was only just enough light to read the words. They were *"SLOW, SLOW, QUICK QUICK, SLOW"* followed by six derisive question marks. Nothing more. No signature. But it was enough. It was her way of letting him know that on this particular Friday, for no reason that he could think of, she had decided to go to the Youth Club dance. And it was because he was so astounded by the news that he'd nearly fallen into Gwen's lap on his way back over the wall.

Well, that was that then, wasn't it? Madge was at the Youth Club dance so he couldn't get hold of her to tell her the news, so he'd just hang about till Gwen came back and then he would tell Gwen and — no, he wouldn't. He could just imagine Gwen's scorn and knew it would be righteous. She had a very effective line in righteousness, Gwen had.

He could choose then between the rough edge of Gwen's tongue and going into the Youth Club dance and fetching Madge out. She'd come at once when she heard. Well then, why not go in? It would mean he'd have to pay, he supposed. But he had the money, he'd started saving for Christmas.

Without giving himself any chance to change his mind, Matt marched into the Youth Club and slapped his money down in front of the man who was sitting at the door. It wasn't a den of lions, other people came out unscathed. In five minutes he'd have done it. He went forward.

The warmth and noise and brightness that met him was like a gentle slap in the face. He'd been in the Youth Club hall for meetings and P.T. and once when they were showing pictures from the art class at school. But this was different.

Matt drew a deep breath of unexpected joy. This was what he'd felt ages ago at the Pantomime in that moment of moments when the orchestra climbed to its close, the house lights dimmed and at last the curtain went up. Everything here was bright and unreal and beautiful. Everything moved, the strange handsome creatures on the floor, the band with Sidney in command, the streamers, the bunches of glossy balloons rubbing against each other in the current of air. The floor below his feet seemed to move. The beat of the music was hot on his face like waves. Fragments from a hundred conversations made him deaf. The mouths that weren't talking were laughing.

It was when the music stopped and the dancers stood clapping that he remembered what had brought him here. Madge — where was she? She'd stick out a mile among this smart crowd, he wouldn't have any trouble spotting her. She wouldn't be talking or laughing, just glowering and enduring until it was over. It was hard to recognize anybody he knew, let alone Madge. Then he remembered what Madge had told him — she wouldn't be out on the floor with a partner, she'd be sitting against the wall somewhere, scowling under her eyebrows because she was blowed if she'd try to look as if she didn't mind that no one had asked her to dance. He made a brief survey of the girls who were sitting down. They all looked extremely gay and content, chattering like starlings, and none of them was in the least like Madge.

He felt angry with the girls for being so much at their ease in a place like this, and all dressed up the way they were. He'd been at school, he supposed, with most of them, fought with them, made them cry, shrieked insults when they did. Here they were sitting around like queens, expecting him to go dotty about them, spend money on them, lie awake at night, go feeble at the knees when he met them. Well, they had a hope!

There was one girl who reminded him just a little of Madge — she had the right hair and size — Madge glammed up no end if you could imagine it, but of course you couldn't. This girl looked smashing and she knew she looked smashing. She was with a greasy-looking type who was talking all the time and she was lapping up every word. Now they were laughing together. Matt wondered what the joke was. He recognized the greasy-looking type — it was Eddie. And then the girl looked across and saw him — and she waved as if she knew him. She did know him. Confusion poured over Matt's head. It was Madge!

At this moment the band started up again, dancers began to move, and he lost sight of her. He dodged about trying to see where she was. The music broke off suddenly and people seemed to swap partners. The music continued and the dance went on. He spotted Madge. She had a different partner but the same air of unnatural agreeableness. Again the music broke. Madge and her partner were a few feet off. Another boy tapped Madge on the shoulder and said, "Excuse me," and when the music began again she danced with him, wriggling her fingers at Matt over her new partner's shoulder.

Matt's blood was up. Who said there was anything special about dancing? It was easy when you knew how, and now he knew just that. What did Madge think she was playing at, all dolled up? She didn't look half silly. He'd tell her. He stood itching and fidgeting until the next interval in the music, then pranced through the crowd and said, "Excuse me," very loudly and sarcastically in Madge's ear. The other chap got the message and cleared off. Matt was elated. He started to explain things to Madge but the music interrupted. "Dance, can't you?" Madge said, smiling fiercely. He danced.

It was, he told himself, as good a performance as the next chap's. You just went from foot to foot with a little knee-bending and bottom-shaking in between. First in one direction, then in the other. Nothing to it. Not so easy to talk, though, with Madge leaping about like that.

"Madge," he said when she had moved in his direction. "Listen. This is important. I've got a message."

"Oh, have you," said Madge, backing.

He pursued her. "What on earth have you got your hair like that for?"

Madge laughed and spun round and said was that the message, and Matt said couldn't they stand still for a while, he had things to say and he'd get hiccups if they went on like this, and Madge said dance, you idiot, and he danced.

"What did you come for?" he said.

"To dance."

"But you said —"

"I had to. Cousin Maudie found out."

"Listen," he demanded, but the music stopped and Madge was claimed by another partner. He found himself standing beside a little pink and white girl with very large eyes. She drew a breath and said, "I saw you when you came in you were late weren't you, I said to myself look at him he's big isn't he, so tall. I like boys who are tall, the last boy I went round with was almost as tall as you, not quite but almost, I used to get a crick in my neck, no honest I did I'm not making it up, and he was ever so funny really, you know the kind, everything a bit of a laugh, well that's all right, I suppose, but it gets on your nerves when it goes on, you know the way some people do, and you have to be solemn sometimes, don't you, because after all life is solemn, that's what I used to say to him, life is serious, I said, but he just laughed. I don't suppose you're like that, are you, I expect you're the shy type that's why you aren't saying anything, I'm shy myself really, but I read in a magazine forget about yourself relax and just talk, it said, you soon get over it, I always read my Stars in the magazines, I don't know if you do, boys don't I think, not like girls, anyway last week it said a chance now to make a new acquaintance there's a disappointment in your path too, well, we went to see this film and it was disappointing all right, terrible it was, so perhaps you're the new acquaintance, well, that's nice isn't it —" and then the music dried up and so did she, and someone else claimed her and welcome, and Matt carved his way back to Madge.

"Oh, you again," she said, haughty like a duchess. "Do you have to?"

He waited till they had danced their way to the door. Then he grabbed her wrist and yanked her outside. Luckily the passage was empty. He wasn't altogether prepared for Madge's fury.

"Look," she stormed, "what is all this in aid of? What do you want to come barging in for? Leave me alone, can't you? What's the big idea? It isn't funny, you know. I was getting on all right, wasn't I? Well, wasn't I? You could see. I was a success — me! It was the first time I'd been a success. It's easy when you get the hang of it. I was enjoying myself till you came along —"

Matt was aghast. "Enjoying yourself? Oh, come off it, Madge, you don't mean it, you know you hate all this kind of larking around, you told me so, all that jigging and smiling. And that was a right weedy specimen you were being so civil to, I must say. What was Eddie on about anyway, he never had much to say for himself." He enjoyed talking to her like this, but the back of his neck prickled uneasily. It was like talking to someone you knew quite well, only the person was wearing a mask. You knew it was a mask, it must be a mask, and yet it moved and spoke — and its likeness and unlikeness to the person underneath was frightening.

The mask smiled and said, "You don't know much, do you, Matt?"

"I'll tell you something you don't know," he snarled at her. "That's if you come down from up there and listen. Pa Flint has had an accident — he's hurt — he's in hospital."

It worked right away. There was no mask, there was only Madge. "Pa Flint? Then why couldn't you have said so at once? You are a blithering idiot, Matt, going on like that. What happened? Why did you have to waste time?"

It was such a relief to have Madge back to normal that he didn't bother to argue. "Anyway, how do you know?" Madge demanded.

"It was Gwen. She saw the stretcher being carried in to Casualty."

"Is he badly hurt?"

"Gwen didn't know. She said he was unconscious."

"Where is Gwen now?"

"Gone back to the hospital."

"What for?"

"She's going to try to get a message through to Mr. Flint to tell him not to let on to the people at the hospital about Ma Flint not being at home. Otherwise Gwen says the Cruelty people will come and organize."

"They would, too, that's why they mustn't come. We've got to see they don't."

"Yes, but how?"

Madge gave him a look of scorn. "We've got to find out how. Come on, we'd better hurry."

She dived into the Ladies to get her coat and reappeared with it slung round her neck, the sleeves flapping. The man at the table beside the door seemed surprised at their departure. "Going already? Any minute now it'll be time for the balloons." "You can tell them from me what to do with them," Madge snapped inelegantly, and swept past like a tornado. Her hair was coming down, lying on her shoulders like seaweed when the tide goes out.

All the way up the street she preached sideways at Matt. "They mustn't split up the family, you must see that, Matt, it's terribly important. They mustn't."

"I thought you didn't mind much about families, that's what you said anyway."

"Of course I mind!"

"Then why —"

"And she could come back any day now. You know she always comes back in the end."

"Well, you could explain that to the Cruelty people, couldn't you?"

"And have the police out scouring the country for her? And in the newspapers and on the radio? Poor Mrs. Flint, what would she feel like, it's her own business if she wants to go off for a bit, isn't it? You can't bring it all up in public, and how do you suppose Mr. Flint would feel?"

"I suppose he wouldn't like it," Matt agreed humbly. His head was spinning.

"He'd never get over it, he's such a quiet little man. And there's Sammy, he's what matters most of all."

"Why Sammy more than the others?"

"Oh, you know! Sammy's different. The Cruelty people would spot it at once."

"You said he wasn't different."

"I don't mean what you mean, but he's different all the same. He needs to be with people who understand about him. It would be terrible for Sammy if they took him away."

"Supposing Mrs. Flint doesn't come back and Mr. Flint has to stay in hospital for months and months? Or he could die."

"He won't," Madge said with flat certainty.

"The neighbors will know if there's no one to look after the family."

Madge turned to look at him. The streetlights made her face brilliant. "There will be someone," she announced, and quickened her pace.

Matt followed. He didn't like the way this was going. He couldn't match Madge's enthusiasm with any of his own. You let yourself think things mattered and got steamed up about them and in the end they didn't matter or it was no use anyway and you felt a fool.

Before they turned the corner he said to Madge, "What was Eddie going on about to you, anyway?"

Madge paused. "Oh — him!" For a moment the warrior fierceness faded from her face.

"Well, what was it?"

"My hair. He said he liked it."

Matt crowed rudely. "He — what?"

"I told you."

"That was a laugh."

The light of battle returned to Madge's eyes. "Come on — there's Gwen — she's waiting!"

⌖ 6 ⌖

THE man in the white coat at the other side of the grocery counter tied up the block of cheese as meticulously as if it had been a bar of gold, sighed as he placed it in front of Matt, and said, "And the next item, sir?" like Hercules signing on for another Labor.

The negotiations for the cheese had occupied several minutes. Cheese, Matt had said, expecting cheese. Ah, but which cheese? It wasn't as easy as all that. You didn't just say "Cheese." There was a great variety of cheeses — which did he require? The man rhymed off the alternatives; they narrowed it down to Cheddar, which on inspection looked more like cheese as Matt knew it than some of the others; and then they debated the question of mild or tasty. "Tasty," Matt said firmly, determined not to lose a match point. He accepted the parcel and added it to those already in his string bag. He heard it drop sickeningly on top of the bag of eggs (large, standard, small, fresh, farm, free-range?) and pretended he hadn't noticed.

The final item on the list which Madge had given him was bacon. "Bacon," he said, "a pound," daring the man to raise complications. The shop had filled up since he'd come in. Already other shoppers were jostling round him; one woman was breathing down his neck and pushing her bag of assorted parcels into the small of his back in a meaningful way.

The man's eyes narrowed. What kind of bacon? Back, shoulder, streaky — ?

"Back," Matt decided.

"*Best* back?" The man found it hard to believe.

Matt's firmness wavered. "I'm not sure."

"What kind did your mum say then, love?" inquired the woman with the parcels.

"She didn't."

"If it's best back he wants, it's best back he shall have," the man pronounced, whisking up a cut from its hook.

"I should take streaky if I was you, love," the woman prompted, "better value with streaky."

"Streaky then," Matt said. With all those Flints to feed, value was what was needed.

The man hung the cut up again and lifted a couple of thinner cuts with patient fury. "White or green?"

Matt was startled. *Green* bacon?

"Take the green," said his self-appointed adviser. "The white looks nothing but fat."

"Green." He was relieved to see that the bacon which had been selected was pink and white after all.

"Make sure it's what you want, love," came the voice from the rear. "Don't let him rush you."

The man had heard. He extended the striped lump

across the counter and held it under Matt's nose. "All right, is it?" He challenged criticism. Matt nodded mutely. Yes, it was all right.

The man impaled the meat on the slicing machine. "Thin or thick?"

"Thick," he guessed.

"Is that what your mum said?" But he pretended he hadn't heard. The machine went into action, the revolving knife sank into the meat. Slices of pink and white streaky bacon grew like flowers from the lump and were whisked away and slapped onto a piece of paper.

He was glad bacon was the last item on the list. It had all taken much longer than he'd expected. Madge and Gwen would be leaping mad wondering where he was. Already he could hear them at it and felt a tug of revolt. This was Saturday morning, they'd been looking after the Flint family for a week — it seemed like six weeks. It had all sounded a lot easier than it was. When you had to spend so much of your life just on the sheer mechanics of living you wondered how anybody ever did anything else. By the time you had thought and shopped and cooked and eaten and cleared up and washed and dried and ironed and swept a bit, there was hardly any time left to be. They were all tired. Even Gwen was tired. Even Madge.

The young Flints weren't tired. This was a pity. It would be easier if they had been. This was the first time Matt had been trusted with the marketing. Other days Madge had bought what was needed at the supermarket where she worked. But today she had begged a day off from work and the girls had conspired together to do a real substantial cleaning, washing, and mending in the flat. They were yakkittying away like a couple of Women's Magazines about a cake they planned to make. The air was thick with plotted recipes. So Matt had been sent out with the shopping list.

He had purposely avoided shopping at the grocer's beside the Flats. The man there knew him and all his mother's shopping habits — there would have been no need to state a choice, but the grocer might ask his mother next time she called whether she'd suddenly had a regiment billeted on her. The supermarket was a long way off and double rations were needed for the week-end — he didn't want to lug them so far. So he'd chosen this shop, not realizing till he was inside how smooth it was. He should have gone to the supermarket even if it meant a walk; there you could rootle around and pick things up and look at them and see if they looked like the things you were trying to buy.

The grocer was handing him the bill. The crowd of women stirred at his back. He was pierced with sudden terror that he wouldn't have enough money; that would be the ultimate shame. Luckily he had enough money; there was tuppence change.

In one way he hadn't been sorry to be so busy all week because there was no time left to scheme or worry about Shaky. And shopping, though it had its hazards, was certainly preferable to Flint-minding. He had shared that with the girls in the evenings during this very long first week. "What do I have to do?" he asked

Gwen before his first spell of duty. "Do? Oh — nothing, really, just be there," Gwen said, sweetly vague. It sounded simple. "When they come back from school keep them in the flat. If they get about outside they'll tell the neighbors. Give them bread and butter till we get back," Gwen added. So he had taken his homework along to the Flints' with him, to pass the time. The girls visited Mr. Flint in hospital and brought him his Savings Book so that he could sign for them to take housekeeping money out of the Post Office, and took sheets to the launderette on the proper day and left out the rent for the Rent Man and finally cooked tea and rounded up the Junior Flints and stowed them in bed, leaving breakfast ready.

But Matt hadn't as much as opened his books in the Flints' flat. He soon found out that what was really required there was an umpire. The very sight of him triggered off in the tribe a kind of cheerful warfare against him and each other. They yelled and banged and chased and laughed and hit and rolled on the floor, singly and in combination. They threw things and jumped up and down on other things. The younger ones clamored nonstop for the lavatory. Sometimes they howled. Sometimes they spat. Sometimes they bled. People in neighboring flats knocked and shouted. It was continuous bedlam until Madge or Gwen showed up. Then the tribe called a truce. The girls were surprised when Matt complained he hadn't got his homework done. "Well, what *were* you doing, then?" they asked crossly. The assembled Flints stood around and smiled.

Yesterday his form master had called him up to his desk after school. Why hadn't he handed in his physics exercise this week? Matt stared, dredging around for an answer that would pass. The waiting master studied him. "It isn't like you, Matt; you're a good worker. You aren't feeling one degree under, are you? Finding the pace a bit much, perhaps?" This unexpected concern roused in Matt's tired brain an impulse to tell him all about it, to let an adult in on this mess. He had respect for this man. He would hand all his worries over to him, Shaky, the Sinister Salesman, the case of the orphaned Flints. Adults were qualified to worry, they had practice.

"Well, sir, you see —" he began, but the master was already gathering up his papers. "We must have a good pow-wow one of these days, you and I," he said, giving Matt one of the keen, soul-stripping glances he made a specialty of (Henry could do them to the life). "You must tell me if there's anything on your mind, boy, that's one of the things I'm here for — eh boy — eh?" and he slid his papers into his case and went off briskly to spread compost on his rose bed.

As Matt had expected, Gwen and Madge were anxious to know why he'd been so long, to tell him he'd brought home too little change and the wrong kind of cheese. But they didn't go on about it as fiercely as he'd feared. Their voices were edgy. He had a feeling things on the domestic front hadn't proved smooth. The girls looked untidy and cross. Madge's lower lip stuck out. Gwen's face was pink, her eyelids their native color.

There was a smell of burnt milk and a black place on the stove. The floor was gray with spilt flour, criss-crossed with footmarks. A row of sodden socks, dripping from the toes, hung on a string above the sink. Madge was scraping away doggedly at the milk saucepan; the drips from the socks went down her neck.

"Why couldn't you have squeezed them some more before you hung them up?" she grumbled to Gwen. Gwen on her knees with a bucket and cloth was starting work on the floor. She looked huffy and said, "I did squeeze. I squeezed all I could."

"Anyway, they aren't rinsed properly. All soapy. You can tell from the drips, they're pale blue."

Gwen was framing a reply when she saw the gluey mess of egg oozing from the bottom of Matt's shopping bag onto an area of floor that she had already wiped. "Matt! What have you done?"

She rose and tried to wrench the bag away from him, but the egg had made the floor slippery and she fell. Her foot caught the bucket — the floor was aswim. One of the Flint children laughed appreciatively.

Gwen picked herself up and was opening her mouth to speak when the cake in the oven declared it had been there long enough. The reek spread through the kitchen. Madge left the sink and sped toward the oven. "My cake!" The cat got below her feet and let out a screech as it streaked for refuge under the sofa. Sammy, who always wept when the cat did, pursued it, bawling. In the uproar a medium-sized Flint asked if his football jersey was dry yet, and another said he was hungry and when was dinner?

At this moment someone knocked on the door. Across chaos and despair Matt and Gwen and Madge looked at each other. Who could it be? Some added trial? Or perhaps deliverance? The grown-ups are coming, hurray hurray! They recognized the cowardly hope in each other's eyes.

It was Gwen who opened the door. A man was standing there, a man they didn't know. Brisk he was and pleasant — a little too brisk, too pleasant.

"Yes?" Gwen's voice was brave enough but you could hear the wobble at the back of it.

"Is this Mr. Flint's house?"

"Yes but he's not at home just now."

The man smiled. "I know he's not at home. I'm from the R.S.P.C.C.," he said. "Can I come in?"

Gwen grew pinker and seemed to sag. "Yes," she said, "I suppose so. What do you want?"

"It's the Cruelty Man! Ya!" said an older Flint.

"I've been informed that Mr. Flint is in hospital following an accident and that the children's mother is not at home. That's correct, my dear, isn't it?"

"Yes. I suppose so. How did you find out?"

"Oh we get to know these things, it's what we're here for," the man said. "Actually, it was one of the neighbors. Now let me see. Who is in charge?"

Gwen hesitated, on the brink of tears. It was Madge who stepped forward, carefully dodging the egg smears.

She looked like royalty, haughty but very polite. "We
are," she said, "and if there's anything we can do for
you —"

The man's eyebrows rose a fraction. "*You*'re in
charge?" He smiled.

"We're friends of the family," Madge said and
counter-smiled. "Won't you sit down?"

"If I may."

Madge sat down opposite the Cruelty Man. It was like two armies drawn up for battle. The Flint children stood around watching, with the same expression on their faces that they wore when there was a boxing

match on the telly. Any minute now they might start to cheer.

"Well, let me see," the man began. Sammy at this moment came out from behind the sofa. He took a look at the visitor and dashed for Madge. She stroked his hair, keeping his face turned away from the Cruelty Man. That was clever, Matt thought. When Sammy was frightened, you knew by his face just how different he was.

"And who is this little chap?" the man asked. "Come now, you mustn't be shy with me, you know. Come and see what I've got in my pocket."

"His name is Sammy," Madge said, holding the child's shoulder and measuring the Cruelty Man with her eye.

"Come and talk to me, Sammy."

Sammy twisted his head away from Madge and began to chatter in his high-pitched private language.

"What is he saying?" the man asked. "Does he always speak like that?"

"Like what?" Madge's voice was icy cold.

"Of course it's not uncommon and nothing to worry about, but there's always Speech Therapy," the man said. "They get wonderful results. Judging by his size I'd say it couldn't be too soon. How old is he?"

"Six and a half," lied Madge.

"Dear, dear! Six and a half!" the man said, "I can't understand a word. What is he saying?"

"He says he doesn't like you and would you please go away now," Madge said graciously.

The man's face reddened. "Never mind that now," he said. He said something would have to be done, the authorities wouldn't stand for neglect, and meanwhile how were they managing? So Madge told him about the arrangements and how easy it was, nothing to it, really. Matt admired her performance but he thought that with the smell of burning, the floor in puddles, and the dripping socks, she could have sounded less enthusiastic. "It's been quite easy, thank you," she concluded.

The man took a look round the room and smiled. His smile became a menace. "How very kind and plucky of you and your friends," he said. "Still I think it's time we came to the rescue, don't you?"

Moment stretched into moment and no one spoke. Matt was watching Madge. He was praying hard that she would surrender. We've done our best, Madge, you know we have. We've only been at it a week and it's been terrible. I hear those kids yelling when I'm asleep. Rescue he says. Rescue from them is about the most blissful thing I can think of. And look at the money we're using. Mr. Flint isn't going to be too pleased when we go back and tell him it's all gone already. A fortnight, he said it should do. We can't keep this up till he comes out of hospital. Four or five weeks at least, they said. Please, Madge. Please. Let the Cruelty People get on with the job, let them be responsible for a change. Let's have some peace. Let's give in. Please, Madge.

"So we shall have to make plans, shan't we, young lady," the Cruelty Man said. "I shall need details, of course — names, ages, infectious diseases — well, I expect you can give me those. And we'll soon find room for them, we'll fit them in here and there. But we must start making arrangements right away."

The eyes of every member of the Flint family were glued to Madge's face. She got up. She seemed very tall. She threw the tails of her hair back over her shoulders. She didn't say anything right away, just went over to the sink and turned off a tap that was plip-plopping into the milk saucepan, measuring the silence. Then she wiped her hands on the dishcloth, giving each finger careful attention. At last she looked across at the visitor. Matt recognised the expression on her face and every last vestige of hope was sucked out of him.

"It's very kind of you, I'm sure," Madge said, like a queen who doesn't need to thank anybody but does it. "It won't be necessary for you to make any arrangements. I'm surprised whichever of the neighbors it was who told you didn't say anything about it."

"About what, my dear?"

Madge stared at the wall a few inches above the Cruelty Man's head. "It's the children's grannie," she said. "She's coming to stay — tomorrow."

Probably the man didn't hear Matt's grunt of surprise because his own was louder. "The children's grandmother? Coming to stay?"

"That's right," Madge said, "until Mr. Flint is better and out of hospital."

"I'd heard nothing about it."

"Probably not," Madge said kindly.

It took a few minutes for disbelief to melt. At last the

message had gone home and the Cruelty Man decided he could go home too. "I'll look in from time to time," he said, "just to see how things are going along."

"That would be very kind," Madge said.

The man moved toward the door. Sammy cheered up and chattered joyfully. "He says he likes grannie," Madge translated without being asked. Gwen opened the door and closed it after the man had gone.

No one in the room said anything. They stood listening to his footsteps crossing the landing. The lift whined and sighed as it reached the Flints' floor. They heard the lift doors open and close. Now it was carrying him down. Madge breathed a long breath of satisfaction. "Well, that's that," she said. "We did it."

"You did it, it was you, you saved us," Gwen said, all soft and ready to cry. "Oh Madge, you were wonderful."

Matt found his tongue. "Wonderful?" he snarled. "I'm glad you think so. I suppose they have got a grannie?"

He looked round at the tribe. They shook their heads, not a grannie on their horizon.

"Well," Matt said, "all we need now is a spare grandmother with lots of time on her hands, to arrive tomorrow, no questions asked and salary strictly imaginary. That shouldn't be too difficult, should it?" He tried to rally Gwen to his side but she avoided looking at him; she was keeping neutral. "We've just about time to go out and choose one this afternoon," he went on. "Lucky it isn't early closing day. Oh, Madge, you are a clot, a clot of clots!"

All the certainty, all the majesty faded from Madge when he said that. At once she became smaller and tireder and more untidy and ordinary. She looked round at the chaotic kitchen, the uneasy children, at Gwen, and finally at Matt with quiet despair. "Oh Matt, what are we going to do?" And Matt, feeling as if he had been pushed violently from the back, heard himself saying, "It's all right, Madge, it's all right. We'll manage."

So here he was, committed to spending a perfectly good Saturday afternoon on a grannie hunt, compared with which a wild goose chase would have been a piece of cake. After the Cruelty Man left them, the girls fed the Flints and Matt and themselves on hunks of bread and cheese, emptied the cookery failures into the bin (the rice pudding still in its dish because they wouldn't be parted), and gave the kitchen a quick swab round.

Then Matt took command. He directed that Gwen was to speed back to the hospital and tell Pa Flint that a Flint grannie was being appointed and would be coming on a visit. (This was in case the Cruelty Man did any sly checking up at the hospital.) Madge was to stay in the flat with the tribe. The tribe were to behave themselves *or else,* and he, Matt, would go out and bring grannie home. And whoever he brought, it was grannie.

It sounded reasonably convincing when he said it. Gwen breathed admiration and relief. The Flints were obviously awed. He didn't look at Madge. Even ten minutes later, out on the pavement, it still seemed feasible. The pavements were swarming with women, all ages, shapes and sizes, kindly-looking, busy, energetic, obviously the right type. It was just a question of picking the right one and —

In less than half an hour on the pavement, the whole thing had revealed itself as a lunatic mistake. He was cold and he was hungry (there hadn't been nearly enough of that bread and cheese, not with all those Flints stuffing their faces). Apart from the fact that you couldn't accost a strange woman and ask if she'd like to stand in as a grandmother to a troop of unknown children, these women were already occupied. Their hands and minds were full of messages, bundles of laundry, lists, children, prams, dogs. They had places to go and things to do. He hadn't a hope. He'd never had a hope.

He bought a bar of chocolate to dull the ache, and racked his brains to see whether among his own acquaintances he could find a suitable candidate for the post. Not one. His mother worked every day — in any case she'd run a mile from what she'd call "other people's business." Madge's weird Cousin Maudie wouldn't have passed for anyone's grandmother (her hair this month was bright as an August cornfield and her eyelashes were to match). Henry's aunt, Miss Mickle, was as deaf as a row of posts. Slowly the stark truth dawned — you didn't pick grandmothers up out of nowhere. You didn't choose or invite or appoint them.

You didn't even kidnap or press-gang them. Like trees in a forest grandmothers grew. A miracle — that was what he needed.

A long, happy, idle queue was gathering outside the Cinema for the Saturday matinee. "NINETY MINUTES OF SPINE-CHILLING HORROR" the poster said. Matt envied them every second of it. Oh, to sit back in the darkness, chewing and carefree, with nothing to do but listen to your flesh creeping. Someone in the queue waved at him. He thought it was the little pink and white girl from the Youth Club dance. He pretended he hadn't seen her.

At the corner of the street where the shops ended he paused. What was the sense of going on? He would have to return to the Flints' flat and admit his failure. Cold, cheese, chocolate and anxiety made him feel a little sick. Without much hope he prayed for his miracle.

Henry came along, whistling in a minor key. Fat lot of use Henry would be. Anyhow, he'd been avoiding Henry since the night they'd made such inexplicable whoopee in the house in Dove Square, and he thought Henry was doing the same. But now Henry stopped alongside as if he was anxious to match Matt's gloom with his own.

"Hallo," Henry said, and Matt said, "Hallo yourself," waiting for him to go on but he didn't. Matt was embarrassed by the memory of their last encounter: Henry shaking a gaping pillow over the banisters to hoarse cries of "Hallelujah!" while Matt put the poker through panes of glass; and the final spectacular slaughter of the umbrella stand.

"Got back all right the other evening, did you?" Henry said in a casual voice, as if the dullness of the afternoon could be brightened if you filled it up with words.

"Yes. Did you?"

"Yes. Heard any more about Shaky Frick since?"

"No. Have you?"

"No."

Matt had enough troubles on his plate without raking up Shaky. Go away Henry and do your worrying somewhere else — but Henry didn't go. They stood swapping sentences, only half hearing what the other was saying, like throwing a ball just because it happens to be there, not because anyone minds about it.

"That Sinister Salesman you were on about," Henry asked. "What's he like?"

"Big chap, bit of a swagger, carries a shiny brown case with him, smiles with his teeth."

"That's him, then."

Matt asked "What do you mean, that's him?"

"Saw him the other day, giving sweets to Sammy Flint — you know, the dim kid."

"He isn't all that dim."

"Anyway, they weren't on the same wavelength."

Matt didn't dispute this. Henry said where had Matt been since, where had everybody been, he hadn't seen Gwen (now he came to think about it) all week, and

Matt asked was he looking for her, and Henry said no why should he be, it was just that he hadn't seen her, and then conversation flagged, though they remained glued together, as flat as the pavement.

Matt asked if Henry was going to the ice rink this evening seeing it was Saturday, and Henry said maybe, he hadn't made his mind up yet, and Matt said he'd have to push on now but didn't move, and Henry asked what was he doing anyway, and Matt said as a matter of fact he was looking for the Flints' grandmother, and Henry said he didn't know they had one, and Matt said no, they hadn't, that was the trouble, and Henry said so what, and Matt said so nothing, he'd have to go now, and Henry said, "Be seeing you then, and the best of British luck to you," and Matt said so long and stayed where he was, in case the grannie-miracle was just round the corner.

"About Shaky," Henry said, as if Shaky was a sore tooth to which his tongue constantly returned. "I've been thinking."

"People do sometimes."

"Somebody ought to do something."

"Such as?" If Henry went on like this, someone would have to do something about Henry.

"Oh, I don't know. There must be something. You said he said if ever you saw Miss Harrison you were to give her his regards."

"Well, I haven't seen Miss Harrison."

"I have," Henry said unexpectedly. He said he'd done a bit of sleuthing round the block of flatlets where people who lived on their own were housed, and he'd seen her coming out. She looked just the same as she used to in Dove Square, he said, and he supposed he could have given her Shaky's message, but he hadn't because it seemed a bit odd, and now he wished he had. "I mean," he went on, "it wouldn't have done any harm, would it?"

Matt didn't answer. He had heard little except Miss Harrison's name and he was afraid to speak right away, because the distant hint of a suspicion of a possibility of a miracle was creeping warmly through the soles of his feet and he didn't want to take any chances by noticing it too soon. Easy does it. Don't rush a miracle.

"So I thought perhaps if you came along with me, we could think up what to say to her," Henry concluded.

Matt said, "We don't have to think!" Organ music, fireworks and brass bands already competed uproariously inside his head. "I know just what to say to Miss Harrison! Oh, Henry!"

Henry stared and said, "Are you bonkers?"

And so Matt told him everything: about Mr. Flint's accident, Mrs. Flint's absence, the ghastly week he'd put in do-gooding with the girls, the Cruelty Man's visit and his battle with Madge, Madge's rash announcement about the nonexistent Grannie Flint, his own rasher promise to produce one, and his fruitless search.

Henry listened. A glimmer dawned in his sluggish eyes. "You are bonkers. What on earth did you say you'd do that for?"

Matt explained he didn't know, he'd said it without

thinking, he imagined it was something to do with Madge — she looked so helpless.

Henry let out a hoot of rude laughter. "Helpless! Madge? You know Madge is just about as helpless as a tribe of gorillas on the warpath!"

Matt didn't argue. Why bother? Everything he said would be all right from now on.

"Light is sown for the righteous and gladness for the upright in heart," Henry intoned happily. "Come on — I'll show you where she lives."

7

THE caretaker at the block of flatlets where Miss Harrison — alias Grannie Flint Designate — lived told them which number was hers, and standing outside the door, Matt and Henry believed so firmly in the fulfillment of their hopes that they cocked an ear to see if they could hear the whirr of Miss Harrison's sewing machine, or the notes of the out-of-tune piano on which she had first played for them the tune of "St. George's Edinburgh." Either would have been a fair omen. But when they knocked no one came, and when they knocked again and listened there was no sound of anyone stirring inside.

"She's out, that's all," Henry said, defying Matt to question their inspiration. From the door on the other side of the landing a woman's head appeared in a hair net and rollers. "Not here," it said briefly.

"Do you know where she is?"

"Along at the Church Hall, likely as not," the head said. "That's where she mostly goes," and withdrew.

"Church? On Saturday?" Matt said doubtfully.

"I expect they have a Pray-In. Come on."

The Church Hall was a small, rather bleak building

(oh, poor Miss Harrison) but there were lights in the windows. "We told the Bishop we'd shout for new churches when we moved out," Matt said uncomfortably. "Remember? Somehow we didn't." The doors opened and women came out, most of them walking singly, most of them elderly, most of them in dark decent clothes.

"I don't suppose anybody'd have listened anyway," Henry said, "and we'd look a right couple of Charlies in this little lot." Matt's qualms of conscience were forgotten and hope burned brightly. All of these women were definitely in the grandmother class. Henry and he had come to the right place.

Miss Harrison, when she appeared, was so like the other women that they hardly distinguished her. Even when she came quite close Matt couldn't be absolutely

sure. Of course it was Miss Harrison — and yet —"It is,"
urged Henry, prodding. "Go on. Say something."

Matt stepped forward. "Miss Harrison." His voice was
creaky. "Excuse me, Miss Harrison."

The woman stopped, peering at him. Then she
smiled and at once became Miss Harrison.

"Matt! Matt McGinley! And Henry Mickle!"

Matt's tongue was paralyzed. Hoarsely Henry said,
"We thought it was you. We weren't quite sure."

"I wasn't sure either," Miss Harrison said. She pushed
the wisps of hair back below her hat; they wondered
how they could have ever doubted that this was Miss
Harrison. "It's lovely to see you both," she said, her thin-

nosed face jerking in an odd kind of way. "My, how big you've both grown!"

"Well, it's more than two years," they said awkwardly, not wanting to tell her that she had shrunk; and Miss Harrison agreed: "Of course it is. Fancy running into you like this!"

Matt swallowed and said that actually they had been looking for her.

"Splendid, splendid," said Miss Harrison and blew her nose. "Are you coming home to tea?"

The comfort of tea with Miss Harrison tempted them. Matt's stomach clamored at the mention of food but he thought of Madge and said stoutly, "Not for tea, thank you very much, but could we ask you something?"

"Animal, Vegetable or Mineral? People don't play that any more except on the radio which isn't nearly such fun; we used to enjoy it so much. All the way to school and back with bulls'-eyes or acid drops tucked into our cheeks. What is it you want to ask?"

Henry cleared his throat in a meaningful way and his elbow got busy again in Matt's ribs.

Matt drew a deep breath. "Do you like living where you are now, Miss Harrison?"

"Like it?" Miss Harrison lifted a speculative eyebrow. "Are you engaged in one of those social surveys you read about and shall we all get our names in the newspapers? Well, that would be splendid."

"No, it isn't that," Henry said. "We just wondered. I mean they're very laborsaving and all that, I suppose."

"So laborsaving that you treasure each separate speck of dust as a personal friend."

"And self-contained, of course."

"So self-contained it's almost a fulltime occupation," Miss Harrison agreed, and added, "Inch-plants make such wonderful companions." In the evening air her sigh appeared as a small white cloud.

Matt accepted this as his omen. "The Flint family, you remember them," he said, running it all together so that it could be said more quickly. "Mrs. Flint isn't at home just now and Mr. Flint is in hospital, he's had an accident, and the man from the R.S.P.C.C. has been round and says they're in need of care and protection and they ought to be put into Homes, but it would be all right if they had a grannie or something to take charge and they'd most probably have to go into different Homes because there are such a lot of them, and Madge and Gwen and I tried taking charge ourselves but it didn't work out and it would only be till Mr. Flint is well again, so we thought — we thought perhaps —" He came to a full stop. Even with such a long run-up what he had to say was impossible.

"Why, of course," Miss Harrison said, nodding her head very quickly. "Of course — what a splendid idea!"

"You mean —?"

"So very clever of both of you!"

"You really mean — ?"

"All my life," Miss Harrison said, "I have wanted to be a grandmother."

They stared, hardly daring yet to be grateful.

"Can you come right away?"

"I shall instruct my nonexistent secretary to cancel every one of my nonexistent engagements as of today," Miss Harrison said briskly.

"Come on, then!"

Each of them took her by an elbow and they conducted their prize in triumph back to the Flats. There was a profound silence in the kitchen when they opened the door. Every eye was hooked on Miss Harrison's face. Some of the younger eyes were pink with crying.

"Grannie!" Matt announced. "This is her! She's come!"

They welcomed her bodily.

Half an hour later, and years and years younger, Matt stepped out on the pavement, leaving Grannie Flint installed. Madge was with him. Henry and Gwen had melted off earlier.

Madge halted, breathing in luxuriant breaths of freedom. "We did it! We actually did it! I was afraid we wouldn't."

"So was I."

"I would have gone stark staring mad in another couple of days," she said. "Doing good is terrible, really. And you feel horrible, hating it so much. You think it should make you feel beautiful and good but it doesn't. All those kids yelling and arguing and being hungry all the time. And having to think what to eat and what we'd got to eat and if there'd be enough. And those beastly saucepans and those socks! It was only a week but it felt like years!"

"Years and years, but they'll be all right now. All we have to do is the messages and the launderette and visiting Mr. Flint."

"Even Sammy," Madge said, "did you notice? He went to her right away."

The pleasure of idleness wrapped them round. In front stretched the city and the empty evening, all theirs. The Flats were behind them. To the west the rooftops and treetops and chimneys climbed in their familiar sequence to the tower of the University, every shade of gray and purple against a clear primrose sky. No clouds at all except on the horizon, lying in heavy bars. One early star. Threads of smoke rising from fires newly lit. People were coming home. All over the city families became complete.

Matt was restless with elation. It was impossible for them to go home before they had celebrated. "Come on," he said. They set off. The air was cool, spiced with coming frost, the pavement under their feet was elastic. Their tiredness dropped off them.

They heard the wail of music as they passed the Cinema. Inside, the final tide of horror was almost at its peak. The street was empty.

As they went past the Post Office, Madge looked over her shoulder and slowed. "Who's that?"

"Who do you mean?"

"That man in the doorway. Over there. I think he's watching us."

Matt looked round. It was a figure he knew, the figure of the Salesman. He had left the doorway and was moving smoothly in their direction.

"Come on!" Matt wondered if he imagined that as they quickened their pace the man's pace quickened to match it.

"Is he anybody you know?"

"I've seen him around, that's all."

As soon as they reached the corner they began by common consent to run. They didn't look back until they had reached the next corner. There was no sign of the man but they went on running.

They were near the park. The bell at the park keeper's lodge was ringing to show that the gates would soon be closed. They fitted the pattern of the strokes of the bell to the pattern of their footsteps, guessing how far they would be able to run before the final stroke. The bell stopped just as they drew level with the gates.

The last of the stragglers from the park were coming through. The park keeper chivvied them as if they were a flock of dawdling fowl. They were giving him cheek, and he was short-tempered. He had come out onto the pavement after them. There was a scuffle and the sound of keys falling, then laughter and more shouting, and a scraping noise as the keys were passed skillfully from toe to toe in the crowd. The man's voice protested; he stumbled in search of his keys. Through the gap in the half-closed gates the expanse of empty park beckoned.

"Come on," Matt said, and they were through and running. The sound of their feet on the gravel was obscured by the rowdy game on the pavement. Now they had reached the grass. Its coldness struck through their shoes; already the blades were springy with frost and gave purchase to their stride.

They came to the bushes at the far side of the grass and pulled up, fighting for breath to exult with. Birds in the branches set up an inquiring complaint. The sound of the uproar at the gates still reached them faintly. The air was filled with the smell of evergreens and winter grass and of a dying bonfire whose smoke hung whitely beyond the roofs of the greenhouses.

Rather than take the path round the bushes they walked through them, arms spread like swimmers breasting the water until it becomes deep enough to swim. Now they had arrived at the stretch of asphalt where the swings and roundabouts were. The park keeper had twisted the chains of the swings together; they hung unevenly in adjacent pairs.

Matt untwisted the chains of the first pair and set them free. He caught one of the seats as it came back toward him. "Come on!"

Madge claimed the other swing. They crouched on the seats, Matt facing one way and Madge the other, competing which of them could first gain height. It was years since Matt had been on a swing but the rhythm of it soon returned — his whole body was working. He urged his swing higher and higher. Now they were both swinging at the highest limit of the chains, reaching the peak of the swing, then coming down through the air towards each other, passing within inches and repassing on the return journey, greeting each other with a whoop each time they crossed on the forward swing.

The sky had changed now from primrose to deepest orange. Bands of light broke through the low shutters of the clouds, turning everything they reached to gold. In his flight the shifting pattern of the branches rushed across Matt's eyes; stars appeared briefly and disappeared. Somewhere at the back of his head he knew there was a moon. Each time he passed Madge he felt the sucking current of air, heard the creak of her chains and her quick intake of breath.

Now they had matched the rhythm of the swings so that they kept time with each other, rising and falling, neither gaining an inch on each flight. No more breath for whooping, but they smiled as they passed because what they were doing was excellent and perfect and could go on forever.

Across the grass came the dull clang of the park gates. The man had recovered his keys and was locking up for the night. Madge heard it, knew what it meant, and her concentration was broken. Her swing lost a few seconds and lagged behind.

Matt shouted, "You're scared!"

"I'm not scared!"

"You are! I saw!"

Madge struggled to regain the lost rhythm but Matt forced his swing ahead of hers, laughing. With all his strength he pushed his swing up into the sky, trying to gain a whole flight on Madge.

A pencil of light was moving toward them across the

grass. Someone was shouting angrily. The park keeper. The game was over.

At once they braced their wrists and ankles to break the pace, and the swings slackened. As soon as they judged it safe, they jumped for it. The asphalt as he landed on it stung the soles of Matt's feet and jarred his ankles. One of his hands went down and the palm of it was grazed. The ground below him rocked; the world was tilted; he felt giddy and found he couldn't stand.

The man suspected where he was — he was walking toward him. With a great effort Matt steadied himself and began to run. He plunged for the bushes, this time crouching down low in them, his face and hands taking punishment. He thought he heard a rush of feet across the grass and imagined a moving shadow. Perhaps it was Madge, perhaps she had got away.

Idiot that he was, he had made himself a prisoner in the bushes. The park keeper swung his torch slowly. The beam of light moved along, probing like a finger into the densest parts of the foliage.

"I've got you," the man's voice said. "Come on out. I know you're there."

Matt froze, keeping his head bent so that the light wouldn't shine on his face. His hair and clothes were dark — perhaps he had a chance. The smell of bruised laurels got up his nose. All his willpower was bent on calming his breathing.

"Just as you like," the park keeper said, "but I can stay here all night, time no object."

Any minute now the light would find him out. He

waited to be discovered. It was like waiting to be hit. Then from the far side of the grass where the railings bounded the street he heard a thud, a loud jeering halloo, a confused sound of running and a second shout. The railings had presented no problem to Madge. She had beaten him to it. "Helpless as a tribe of gorillas on the warpath," Henry had said. Henry had got something there.

The park keeper swore and turned in the direction of the lodge, believing that he had been mistaken and that both his quarries had got away. His footsteps diminished as he crossed the grass, the torch flickering ahead of him.

When he judged it was safe, Matt came out from the bushes. He was cold and his face was scratched, he had twigs down his neck and in his hair, and his grazed hand stung. Madge could be halfway home by now, unscathed. He dodged the thought that he owed his own escape to her. Madge had a way of putting things the wrong way round. Irritated and with his head still swimming, he crossed the grass. When he saw the light go up in the window of the lodge he negotiated the railings and dropped into the street. He was glad to find Madge hadn't waited for him. He might have had to be grateful.

Fifteen minutes later he entered the block of Flats

and crossed the hall. He didn't notice, just inside the door, the lounging figure which became alert as he passed and followed him into the lift. It was only when he felt the floor of the lift tilt as the man entered it that he glanced round and saw who it was. The lift doors shuddered and drew together. Matt put out his hand to press the number nine button. A larger hand came over his shoulder, brushing his hand aside, and a finger fastened on the button for floor seventeen, the top floor in the block.

"Aim high, son, always a good motto," he heard the Salesman's voice say. "Nothing like going straight to the top."

Matt turned and snapped, "Look, it's number nine I want — I live there."

"I know," the Salesman agreed. "I visited you there a week or so back — remember? My my, that's a face you've got there, you've been getting the worst of it, haven't you? Has nobody ever taught you how to look after yourself, son? Time you were learning."

Matt was too angry to answer. Outside the gates of the lift successive landings were now dropping away like cards in a skillfully shuffled pack.

"Last time we met, son, we had quite a chat."

They reached floor seventeen and the lift settled and sighed. The doors opened. Matt waited, aching for the man to get out. He didn't move. He was standing now with one arm extended across the open door. It wasn't by accident that his arm was there. Matt realized this and for a giddy moment of panic thought of ducking below that arm and reaching the landing. But the doors had closed again and again the hand of the Salesman got there first and pushed the button marked "Basement." The lift responded and began to descend.

"I saw you going off this evening," the Salesman said, "and I thought I'd like to have another chat, so I hung around till you got back. You told me you didn't like the Flats as much as the place you'd lived before, remember? Dove Square, you said."

"I didn't say it was Dove Square."

"Didn't you? That girl you were with this evening — she lived in Dove Square too, did she? One of your old friends?"

"What girl?"

The man sighed. "Oh, come off it, son. The girl with red hair."

Matt stared mutely at the procession of floors that rose and disappeared. He prayed that on some landing someone he knew might be standing and he could make a signal to them. But what kind of a signal? "Help! Get me out of here!" They'd think he was crackers. In any case the landings were empty. Most of the people who were going out for the evening had already gone and the people left behind had settled down for the three-hour goggle. He was stuck in this cage.

"Lives with her mother, does she?"

"Who?"

"That girl."

"No. She lives with her cousin." It was satisfying to prove him wrong. Matt saw the trap just too late.

"Ah. Which block of Flats? One of these, is it? Which floor?"

The lift flashed past the entrance hall and sank to the basement. This was where the fuel stores were, the rooms with washing machines and spin driers, deserted at this time of the evening.

"That's all I want to know," the man said. "You tell me which block of Flats, which floor, and I'll punch number nine button straight away and send you home to mum. And if — *if* you should happen to make a mistake and tell me the wrong address I can quite easily come back and ask again, can't I? It isn't likely you'd make the same mistake twice."

Matt ignored the silky threat and said, "Why don't you ask the caretakers? They have the names of all the people who live in the Flats."

"I have asked."

"Well, then, they don't live in any of these Flats."

"People don't always have the same name, do they?"

Matt didn't answer. Faintly from some distant floor over their heads the lift bell buzzed. He burned with gratitude. The lift doors had started to close. The Salesman shifted his position, leaning a shoulder against one of the doors. The door hesitated, then reopened. Matt saw his chance and jumped for it but the man's arm went across and pushed him back. "No sense in being awkward, son. Let's just finish our talk, shall we?"

Matt tried to avoid looking at the man's face; he wished they did not need to stand so close. "Why do you want to find these people, whoever they are?" he said, trying at the same time to avoid a private guess.

"I've been away, that's why. Now I'm back it's only natural I want to look up old friends, say hallo, pick up some gear I left with them."

"Perhaps these aren't the right people."

"And perhaps they are."

"Where have you been anyhow?"

The bell buzzed but the man's shoulder prevented the lift from closing. "Out of the country."

"How long have you been away?"

"Does it matter? A dozen years, I suppose, maybe more."

"These friends of yours — didn't they tell you when they changed their address?"

"Maybe they tried to. I was moving around. I was never much of a letter writer, you know the way it is." The man waited. The wet smell from the washing machines seeped into the lift.

"All right, then," the man said, "you're no fool, son, are you? I'll tell you. It's a common enough story, I daresay. I'm not the only one. I went overseas to seek my fortune. I had big ideas — well, I wouldn't blame a man for that, would you? It's a poor heart that hasn't. But sometimes a man's luck is against him. You know that, don't you, or have you been one of the lucky ones?"

"No," Matt said, "not always." Inside him a clear rational voice was saying, "Don't be a fool, Matt, you are listening to a hard luck story," but already his sympathies were enlisting on the man's side. Villains, to his knowledge, were successful. They thrived in their villainy before they were brought low. This man hadn't had much in the way of success.

There seemed now to be a bond between them, at least they were on the same wavelength. The man had guessed what he was thinking. "I suppose you think this is a pleasant job, trading this stuff round the doors?" He indicated the leather case that lay on the floor of the lift beside him. "Perhaps you think I like it?"

Matt stammered, "I — I don't know."

"But you can guess. Knocking on door after door and never finding a welcome — it's not much to write home about or be proud of. After a while, no matter how thick your skin is, it does things to you."

"I suppose it does."

"The women look through the window to see who it is and then they send the kids to bawl you out. 'Mum says we don't want anything!' and the door slammed in your face. The kids enjoy slamming the door. Well, I wouldn't blame them."

The bell buzzed. The obedient gate moved, rocked against the man's shoulder and returned to its place.

"That's the time you need friends," the man said, "if you can find them, that is. It's a sad thing to come home and find your friends have gone."

One more minute of this, thought Matt in desperation, and I will take him round to Cousin Maudie's myself and ring the bell and introduce him personally and see he stays for supper. But the man was occupied with the straps of his case. He had opened it. He had taken something out. Now he held it toward Matt.

"This was the one that took your fancy, wasn't it? I've got a good memory. Well, I need to have in this business. And you picked a winner when you fancied this one."

Matt looked at the man's hand. In the palm lay the little watch, the watch with the daisy-like face, so small that the hands were like hairs.

"Pretty, like you said." It was so quiet that the sound of the watch ticking filled the lift. "A nice Christmas present for your Mum — or for anybody else, come to that."

Matt's fingers itched to pick up the watch. "I told you — I hadn't the money — I still haven't."

"Who said anything about money?"

Matt looked at the man and saw he was smiling. This was the way he had smiled at Shaky Frick's gray face while he threatened to turn him out of his home.

"No harm in what I'm asking," the man said. "In fact it would be a kindness — uniting absent friends. Just the ticket for Christmas, don't you think? Well timed — the Season of Goodwill. We can do each other a good turn, you and I. You tell me which block of Flats to look in — never mind the number — and —" He held the watch a little closer.

Matt's anger took hold of his tongue. "You can take your watch and jump off the Suspension Bridge, that's what you can do!" he shouted. "If there's no harm in it why didn't Shaky Frick tell you where they lived when you asked him?" and realized as soon as the words were out the enormity of his mistake.

The man didn't answer at once. He withdrew his hand and put the watch back carefully in its place. He closed the case again and fastened the straps. When at last he looked up he wasn't smiling. "So it was you, was it?"

Matt said, "Yes," and felt sick.

Suddenly the man began to laugh. "I smelled you that night. You reeked to high heaven. God, it was funny! How you smelled!"

Matt ached to hit him, but in these few feet of space he knew he hadn't the ghost of a chance to escape afterwards. Someone on an upper floor had buzzed the lift twice and was now holding a finger on the button so that the buzz was continuous. The lift door struggled to answer; the Salesman still held it back. Far overhead voices were raised. Matt thought they were coming nearer, and hope prickled. On an upper floor someone was thumping the lift gates and shouting.

The man stretched out an arm and hooked his finger into Matt's collar. "So you're a friend of Shaky Frick's, are you?"

"Yes."

The finger pulled him closer. "All right, that's fine. We can do a deal."

Like a fish half-choking on a hook Matt struggled, but the finger held him fast. "Now listen. Are you listening?"

"Yes."

"You wouldn't want any harm to come to Shaky?"

"No."

"Shaky's your pal."

"I told you."

The voices were coming nearer. Now Matt could hear a rush of descending footsteps. How many floors had they still to come? How long would it take them?

"He won't like it, your pal, if he has to turn out of his little home, will he?"

"You know he won't."

"But he may have to turn out if the powers that be find out he's there. And there'd be trouble, you know that."

The hope of rescue made Matt bold. "You wouldn't tell them. You wouldn't dare!"

"Why wouldn't I dare?"

"People might start asking questions about you, mightn't they, and you wouldn't like that. I knew you were only saying it to scare him!"

"I wouldn't be so sure of that." The man put his face close to Matt's. "I wouldn't bet on it. You watch too much telly, that's your trouble. It wouldn't take much to make me split on Shaky, there are ways of doing it, quiet ways. And then he'd be out on the street. Unless — unless someone else tells me what I want to know first — see?"

The voices and footsteps could now be only a few floors away. The man withdrew his finger at last and Matt staggered free. The man took his shoulder and propelled him through the lift gates and out on to the landing. Then he stepped back and allowed the doors to close. "You can choose," he said, speaking through the lattice. "That's fair enough. Either you tell me or he does, it's up to you now. Think about it. Be seeing you, I'll be around!"

The voices and footsteps were coming down the final flight. The man waited until they had almost arrived and then he pressed the button and the lift rose. The last Matt saw of him he was smiling.

Matt had only time to dodge along the passage and crouch down in a doorway. The crowd on the stairs, seeing the lift shoot skyward, turned and hurried back where they had come from, an angry tangled mob getting in each other's way. They wouldn't catch him, Matt knew that. Even the swiftest runner, running downstairs, couldn't beat the lift. So he had given them the slip.

When it was quiet again Matt started for home, deciding to use the stairs. He had been right, the entrance hall was empty. From the street the voices of the first carol singers floated through. "Hark the Herald Angels Sing." He had nine more flights of stairs to climb and he was tired, tired all over. But he hardly felt his tiredness, nor did he hear the song of the Herald Angels because of the clarion call that was now battering his eardrums. This time there was no escape. He'd wanted a Cause; all right, he'd got one.

8

By the end of a week the clarion call had dwindled to a siren that whined perpetually somewhere at the back of his mind. He couldn't shut it out. Sometimes it faded a little, he had almost forgotten it — and then he turned a street corner and saw, or thought he saw, a tall figure strolling toward him, and the siren wailed afresh and sent his stomach leaping with terror. So! The moment had come, the choice would have to be made! But always the tall figure was someone else. Only in dreams was the tall figure really the Salesman come to demand an answer from him, but Matt always woke before he heard his own voice stating what the answer was. He hadn't decided anything. Sometimes he argued the thing through and reached a decision and knew what to do, and then proved his arguments wrong and ended up doing nothing.

Fat lot of good you are, he raged at himself, trying to force himself into some kind of action by insults. Go on — do something, don't just stand about and moan. "There is a tide in the affairs of men" — the school play had been Julius Caesar. But these tactics didn't work. After a few days of it he began to cultivate a deliberate sluggishness, a cotton-wool mind. He read old comics that he dug up from the back of a cupboard when his homework was finished, kept the transistor going non-stop, and spent more than he could reasonably afford on the slabs of toffee that took longest to chew through. His feet were stuck in mud up to his ankles and both the mud and his feet were cold.

He was glad there was enough end-of-term frenzy to keep him outwardly occupied. Exams and Christmas Carol practice and the play helped to crowd out the fear. When school broke up in the middle of December a faint hope had begun to glimmer that perhaps the Salesman wasn't coming back for an answer, that he'd been bluffing, or else that it was his idea of a joke. If he thought about this quickly and often enough, Matt found it possible to believe it was true.

The school holidays were going to be awkward. Not so much to think about, not so much to do, fewer people in whose company to do it. He had realized that the Salesman would only approach him when he could find him by himself. Already Matt was avoiding empty lifts and deserted pavements, and he didn't answer the door when he was in the flat alone. To be alone was danger-ous. "Let me have men about me that are fat," Caesar had said. The trouble with fat people was that they were usually good-natured, the sort of people you would want to tell things to — and the one and only thing of which Matt was now unshakably certain was that he could tell nothing at all to anybody. He must even avoid the temptation of a pair of sympathetic ears.

Once, only once since that evening in the lift had he

seen the Salesman, and the Salesman hadn't seen him. It was in the chemist's. Matt had gone in to buy aspirin for a streaming cold. Henry was there, demanding pre-shave in a lordly voice loud enough for the whole shop to hear.

"What's the matter, old son? Toothache?" Henry asked. "That's what you look like, proper old woe-bag." Matt sneezed in reply. "Ah," Henry said. "Flapping around in a toga and sandals in December — you're asking for it. If you were any good at it you should have had enough dramatic fire to keep you warm."

"I hadn't," Matt said between sneezes.

"I suppose it was the usual load of lisping kids?"

"I suppose so," Matt agreed drearily, and then felt an air colder than any of Imperial Rome, because the shop door had swung open and the Sinister Salesman had come in.

He walked past the little queue of customers and set his case down on the counter and stood there, smiling. Matt, with his pulse playing drums, wheeled toward a rack of toothbrushes and studied them with passionate interest, keeping his face turned away. Hard, Medium Hard, Extra Hard, green, blue, red — these were the vital choices. Henry nudged him. "I say — Matt — look, isn't that —?" but Matt didn't reply.

"Well, what is it?" he heard the chemist inquire irritably, and in the man's pleasant answer heard the smile he couldn't see. "Just thought I'd drop in — some very attractive lines here, quite exceptional, knew you wouldn't want to miss a chance —"

"If you're trade come back first thing in the morning, I have a lot of customers right now." A murmur from the queue agreed with the chemist.

"Just at the right time then, customers, my favorite people!" The man's voice entreated the response Matt knew he wouldn't get. Probably he knew it too, he must know if he'd any sense. Go away why don't you, they don't want you, the chemist doesn't want you. Clear off before you make too big a fool of yourself. Go away decently and quietly. We don't want to be embarrassed by you, it isn't fair on us.

"You heard what I said," the chemist answered. "In any case I only buy from the established houses." There was a rustle of amusement and support from the customers. Quite right, too.

Matt turned from the toothbrushes just in time to see the Salesman's face as he left the shop, just in time to enjoy the chemist's victory and feel excited by it — and then to hate himself. It was wrong for any adult's face to look like that. It was wrong that, if he'd wanted to, he, Matt, could change that look. Maybe after all you're being unfair. Run after him, tell him where he can find his friends and his welcome.

"No use for casual peddlers," the chemist said crisply. "Who's next, please?" Matt bought his aspirin.

There was no sign of the Salesman when he stepped out onto the pavement. From the other side of the street two posters confronted him, the jolly red-nosed Santa advertising his visit to a local store, and a starving child for a charity appeal; they canceled each other out and left a sick empty feeling.

He went to visit Mr. Flint in hospital. The little man looked like a good child tucked up in bed, very tidy and grateful and anxious. Getting on fine at the Flats, Matt told him, Miss Harrison makes a smashing grannie, no hitches anywhere, and the girls are running around like rabbits doing the messages.

"Very kind. Very kind of one and all I'm sure. Much obliged," Mr. Flint said, but his forehead was still puckered with worry. "You find out who your friends are at a time like this." He hesitated, then said, "You mustn't think hardly of her, Matt. I shouldn't like you to do that."

"No. No of course not, why should I?" Matt's face was flaring with embarrassment encouraged by the dry heat of the ward.

"She doesn't have an easy time one way and another. Women don't. And she's been a wonderful wife to me, a wonderful mother to the kids."

Matt tried to dodge those gentle eyes. Why tell me? I'm a schoolboy, I'm still excused from opinions and judgments. Adults are a different breed, what would I know about them? I'm just a kid. I hadn't even a speaking part in the school play, I was only one of the rabble, draped in one of my mum's sheets, bawling with the rest of them what I was told to bawl. He left his two oranges on Mr. Flint's locker and walked away quickly.

Madge was just coming into the hospital to see Mr.

Flint as Matt left it. He'd kept out of Madge's way since that rare and hilarious evening on the swings, but now she stopped to talk. Cousin Maudie had given her money — she must have had a lucky run on her Bingo night — pushed it at her, Madge said, you know what Cousin Maudie's like in one of her Duchess moods, bestowed it on her graciously, lovely money, lots and lots. So Madge was going to the Co-Op to buy Christmas presents for the Flints. Would he come and help her buy? Meet him there in half an hour after she visited Mr. Flint. All right, Matt said, he might as well.

The big shop was crowded and festive. There was a riot of spending in the toy department. Balloons and paper chains and Chinese lanterns hid the ceiling and stirred a little in the heated air. Colored lights flashed off and on outside Father Christmas's Grotto, and gnomes beckoned. A parrot in a cage said, "Happy Christmas" over and over. Lost babies wailed underfoot and were reclaimed. Cash registers rang up the goodwill. Dynasties of dolls closed their eyes and opened them, declaring "Mamma!" On the miniature racing track model cars pursued each other. Supersonic missiles whined through their paces. Batman prowled. Clockwork ran down and was rewound. "Happy Christmas," the parrot said.

"This for Sammy," Madge decided, "this for Pete, this for Winston." They squeaked rival teddy bears at each other until they found the best. Spending money was wonderful — it made you feel good. "We'll go round to the Flints on Christmas morning," Madge declared.

There was still some money over. They plunged into
other departments. Matt felt safe and happy, wedged on
all sides by elbows. No Sinister Salesman could approach
him here. "How much have we got left?" Bath salts for
Ma Flint in case she came back. A tie for Mr. Flint.
They giggled over one with a picture of a dusky South
Sea maiden printed on the lining, and chose a sober one
of heather-colored tweed. Mr. Flint hoped to be out of
hospital next week. Miss Harrison had said she could
stay on till then — everything was working out. Matt's
inner siren signal shrank, no louder now than his own
breathing.

The last of the money had been spent. Madge loaded
up the parcels. She must get home right away, she said;

she was going out later. Feeling easier than he had for days, Matt allowed her to go on ahead and followed at his own pace.

Last week the men had brought the Christmas tree and tipped it off the back of a lorry and left it on the grass in front of the Flats beside the piece of sculpture. It was a poor looking, spindly object lying there with half of its branches flattened and the raw white wood at the base exposed. You couldn't imagine that this tree had ever lived and grown and welcomed birds to its branches, that spiders had ever spun their webs in it, that it had felt starlight or gales or the weight of snow. But since this morning, the men had come back and erected the tree and strung it with decorations, and now the lights in the branches were burning.

Matt was taken by surprise. In the luminous December dusk the tree now lived and grew — not spindly but slender. It breathed spicy forest air. Electric light bulbs and balloons had become strange fruit and blossom. The branches gleamed with spangled swags of silver which moved and swung. Now Matt remembered woods in the country where he had been brought up, and other Christmases when his father was alive, and whole processions of Christmas trees.

Sammy Flint came and stood beside him, talking in his own language and staring at the tree. He caught Matt's hand and pulled it and kept on pulling.

"What is it, Sammy? What do you want?"

Whatever it was, Sammy wanted it badly. "Take your time," Matt advised. "Tell me slowly."

The little boy tried very hard. The colored lights lit his face as he struggled to make Matt understand. He repeated the same noises several times. Matt couldn't make sense out of any of them.

"Sorry, son, it's no good." But Sammy still held his hand and was still pulling. "All right then, why don't you show me?" Sammy brightened and led the way to the shops, chattering all the time.

When they reached the television shop Sammy stopped and anchored himself at the window. Now Matt knew why they had come. This was Friday, the evening for another episode in the horrific serial. The Flint household was still without its telly, so the little boy came to the shopwindow and watched from the pavement. Most Fridays he persuaded Madge to come with him to make the fear more endurable. But Madge had told Matt she was going out tonight, so Sammy had had to look for another escort.

They stood at the window. They were just in time — the serial's introductory fanfare reached them faintly. Sammy's grip on Matt's hand tightened. They watched as the story unfolded. Sometimes Sammy drew in short breaths and exhaled through his teeth when the moment had gone safely past. New and more terrible tensions built up. Behind the glass the mouths spoke words that were inaudible. Matt's hand was aching from the fierceness of Sammy's clutch, but he hardly noticed, for he was chewing something else over unhappily in his mind.

Madge had told him she was going out — she hadn't

said where. She had no need to say — this was the night
of the Christmas Dance at the Youth Club, the crowning
jollity. A few weeks past, in the derelict waiting room of
the station, she'd made eloquent fun of these dances.
Now she'd changed her tune. This time she was going of
her own accord. It was Eddie, of course. Probably at this
moment Madge was brushing her hair in front of her
mirror, smiling at herself and wondering what Eddie
would say about it this time.

The kid was grunting in an odd sort of way. His arm
jerked; his hand was wet and sticky. Inside the television
screen a monster thumped a metal paw into the stomach
of a man. With each thump Sammy grunted. There was
a close-up of the man's face. Again the metal paw came
down. The man went limp.

Then the music spread through the plate glass, the
names of the cast flickered across the screen, and it was

over till next week. The kid at once loosened his hold on Matt. He dodged off without good-bye or thanks and was lost among the eddies of late shoppers.

Matt should have taken him straight back to the flat. Probably Miss Harrison didn't know he was out on the loose, and she'd be worried frantic, but it was no use trying to chase after him now. Matt turned for home, angry with the kid for needing to be frightened, angry with Madge, angry with himself for minding about either of them.

He passed the entrance to the Youth Club. It was alive with lights and he could hear the eager pulse of the band. Already people were going in. A few yards farther on he came face to face with Madge. She was hurrying, her coat was open and he could see the flowery stuff her dress was made of, and her long light stockings.

"Oh hello, Matt," she said without stopping. But Matt stepped out in front of her.

"In a hurry?" he asked. "I don't suppose Eddie likes to be kept waiting."

"Nobody likes it, come to that," Madge said, looking over his shoulder to see if Eddie was lining up for her at the door. "You are a loon, Matt. Why don't you go and get lost?"

"Sammy isn't fond of waiting either," Matt accused, in scalding tones.

At once Madge's eyes came back to him. "Oh, Matt! I'd forgotten about Sammy!"

"That's all right. Nothing to get steamed up about. I went with him."

"All the same, I should have remembered."

"I tell you, it was all right."

Madge didn't move; her face was still stricken. She had no need to take it as hard as that. They were getting in the way of other people, standing there anchored on the pavement.

"I've never forgotten before — not once."

"I tell you it didn't matter. Anyhow you'd better go on, hadn't you?"

Madge pulled back the cuff of her coat and held her wrist up to the streetlamp. "Yes, I suppose I should, it's gone half past."

Matt's hand shot out. "Hi! Let me see that!"

"Be careful, it's new!"

"I want to see it."

It was the watch, the small daisy-faced treasure of a watch. Matt recognized it at once. It gleamed in the light from the streetlamp. The same watch — only on Madge's wrist. Her wrist looked different.

He let go and said, "Where did you get that?"

"What's it got to do with you where I got it?"

"Just tell me, that's all."

"From Cousin Maudie."

"Where did she get it?"

Madge smiled at the watch. "From an old friend of hers, she said. Someone who called. It sounded like the Crown Prince, the way she went on — you know what she's like, all girlish."

He didn't share the joke, and she said, "I don't see it's any business of yours anyway, Matt McGinley."

"Well, go on then," he said. "Why don't you?"

She left him standing there and walked toward the lighted doorway; he waited till she had gone inside. When at last he moved, he knew where he was going and what he intended to do.

"Who is it?" Cousin Maudie's voice called when he rang the bell. A moment later she opened the door. "Oh, it's you, Matt. Surprise, surprise! Righty-ho then, you'd better come along through. I'm doing my face."

She was wearing a dressing gown of shrieking pink, and bedroom slippers. He followed her feathered heels.

Cousin Maudie sat down at the dressing table and went on where she'd left off. In front of her was a litter of tubes and small bottles, of jars and cotton wool and tissues, of lipsticks and pencils, of small fine brushes, lacquers, lotions. There was a drink in a tumbler; she'd been knocking it back a bit, Matt could tell that. A transistor was going full blast. The air was scented. The shaded lamp threw a pink cone of light on the three faces of the mirror and on Cousin Maudie's face reflected in each of them. Matt thought of his mother's dressing table with its prim starched mat edged with crochet, the brush, the comb. The big window beside Cousin Maudie was uncurtained and the city lights were scattered far, far below.

Cousin Maudie's face was covered in a smooth gray-pink paste, she didn't half look silly like that. She moistened a pad of cotton wool and began to clear the paste away, dabbing and looking in the mirror inquiringly, like a short-sighted hen pecking, Matt thought, swallowing his furious laughter.

"Well, go on, what is it?" She glanced sideways at Matt between pecks.

"That watch — the one Madge is wearing — where did she get it?"

Cousin Maudie made a face at her reflection. "Oh that — I gave it to her."

"Who gave it to you?"

Cousin Maudie went all over her face pinching her skin between forefinger and thumb. Then she spread cream on it as if she were buttering bread, and slapped at herself. "It was you, was it? Fancy! I wondered who it was. He said he'd shown it to a boy who admired it."

"I was to have it for a present if I told him where you lived. He tried to bribe me." How pious his voice sounded.

Cousin Maudie laughed. "So that was what he was up to!" She wiped her fingers on a tissue and took a drink from the tumbler.

"Who is he, anyway?"

"Someone I used to know long before you and your mum came to live in Dove Square, if it's any business of yours, which I doubt." She inspected different pencils and did things to her eyelids and her eyes. She made one of her eyebrows longer than the other and took cream and rubbed it out.

"How did he find you?"

Cousin Maudie chuckled. "Funny, that was. He rang

my bell and I opened the door and he was halfway through selling me an apple corer, and then — laugh? I'll say we laughed!"

"When?"

"This afternoon. I was back early from work." Now she had reached a critical stage. When she turned from the mirror he saw that her eyes had become larger and mysterious, fringed with enormous lashes. Like a cow, he mocked silently.

"Look, kid." She consoled him as if he needed comfort. "Not to worry. It's all being taken care of."

"Did he find out where you lived from Shaky Frick?"

"From who?"

"You remember Shaky Frick in Dove Square?"

"The little man with the dogs?"

"Yes."

"Where does he come into it?"

"I wanted to be sure it wasn't Shaky who told him where you lived."

"I said so, didn't I? The bell rang and I went and opened the door and there he was —" She began to laugh again in a silly kind of way.

"What did he want to find you for?"

"Old friends. No friends like old friends, that's what they say, isn't it?"

"And there was the money, of course."

Cousin Maudie switched off the transistor. Their words became more important. "What money?"

"The money he left with you."

"Now see here, Matt McGinley —"

"He told me he'd left something with you — I guessed it was money. Did you give it to him?"

"I told him where he could collect it."

"Under the floorboards at the window, below the lino with the daffodils," Matt said, working it out.

Cousin Maudie swung round. Some of the jars and bottles were caught by her sleeve and went sprawling on the dressing table, knocking into others and taking them down like ninepins.

"What are you talking about?"

"That was where you hid his money."

Now her face was like a clown's face. The eyelashes had become decorations stuck there for fun. Her mouth was a hole.

"Did he ask you to hide it?" Matt said. "Why did he want it hidden? Who is he, anyway? When did he give you the money?" She looked so unreal that it was possible to ask impossible questions. "Well — go on. How long ago?"

Cousin Maudie turned away, staring past her own reflection and out at the lights of the city, though she wasn't seeing them. She was talking to herself, not to him. "Ten years, more than ten. I hadn't seen him for a while and then he turned up in Dove Square late one night, smiling. He always turned up smiling, even when he was in trouble. He was in trouble all right. 'They're looking for me, Maudie,' he said. And then he gave me the money. 'Hold on to this for me, I'll be needing it when I come out. You might even help me to spend it

162

some day,' he said. And he went away. I read in the paper afterward they'd picked him up and he'd got ten years."

"He said he'd been out of the country," Matt objected.

"He was always a good talker. I hated that money, right from the start. I didn't know what to do with it — Madge was only a kid, she had her fingers in everything — anything you hid she found it. So I put it under the floor in the kitchen, where she wouldn't know. And when we were moved out to the Flats I left it there. Let it stay, I said, it's as good a place as any. It'll be a new start for us, at the Flats. He's gone now, I said, we're rid of him. It's all over. And when he comes out he won't find us. But I used to think about that money. I couldn't stop thinking about it. Once when I got behind with the rent I went back to Dove Square and looked under the floor and it was still there, but I knew I couldn't spend it so I left it where it was. The houses were empty but there was no talk of pulling them down yet and the money was safe enough. I knew gangs of boys were wrecking what they could in the old houses, but nobody was going to tear up a whole floor looking for money they didn't know was there, were they? But I still hated it. I wondered if I ought to take it away and burn it —"

"Why didn't you?" Matt demanded.

"I was afraid he might find where we were when he came out. And he'd come to ask where the money was, so that he could collect it."

She lifted a large puff and dabbed at her face. The cone of light from the lamp was filled with a cloud of powder.

"He won't be able to collect it. It isn't there," Matt said.

The powder in the pink cloud had already begun to settle before she spoke. "What do you mean? It isn't there? How do you know?"

"It's been taken. I was there a few weeks ago. The lino was rolled back and the board had been pulled up and left standing. I put my hand in and felt about; there wasn't any money underneath."

She stared at him. "No one knew where it was. No one except me. Unless — I suppose someone *could* have found it by accident."

"Whoever found it knew where to look."

"But I told you. No one else knew."

"You have to believe me," he said. "The money isn't there."

"Then someone found it by chance."

"Chance my foot! You should have seen the room — only that piece of linoleum had been moved, no board except that one. Whoever took the money saw you when you were hiding it, or when you went back afterward."

"Who could have seen me? I was very careful. I went early in the morning; there was no one about. There isn't anyone about in the mornings."

Matt spoke slowly. "Except for Shaky Frick. He's still living there in one of the basements. Madge and I saw him. And your friend knows too. He found out Shaky was living there." Then he felt cold and said, "And when he discovers the money's gone he'll think it was Shaky who took it."

"He's going to Dove Square tonight," Cousin Maudie said. "If he thinks it was that poor little man who took it —"

"Why were you so pleased when he came back?" He didn't know he was shouting till he heard his voice.

"Who said I was pleased?"

"I knew. The way you told me — the way you went on about it — how you laughed when you opened the door and found him outside — of course you were pleased."

"Look, little boy, it's time you grew up a bit, isn't it? When you get older you don't always boo the Baddies and clap for the Goodies — that's something you'll have to learn."

"I don't have to learn he's a twister, anyway."

"You shut up, kid," Cousin Maudie said. "I know everything he is. You don't have to tell me. I know it all."

There is a moment at the circus when the clown stops being something you can laugh at, and without any warning your heart turns over because you know you are going to have to be sorry for him, and you are angry because this isn't fair.

"He only came back for the money, you said that yourself," Matt jeered. "That was why he was so keen to find you."

"Yes. It was only for the money. I knew that all along."

He drew a deep breath and asked, "Did he say the watch was for Madge?"

"Yes."

"Is he her father?"

"Yes." It was her turn to mock. "She has to have one, you know. It's one of the rules."

"Won't he come back because of that?"

"No."

"Madge's mother, then. She might come back."

"No, she won't."

Cousin Maudie stood up. She looked dignified, there was no hint of the clown. Sometimes in the morning when you draw back the curtains it is already daylight outside — flat obvious daylight. You should have known all the time that it was there.

"Why won't her mother come back?"

"Because she never went away."

Then Cousin Maudie opened the door and stood waiting while he went through. When it closed he could hear her laughing or crying, but he couldn't tell which it was.

9

"Boys!" Gwen said gloomily. "I don't know, honest I don't. Remember my big sister — she was always on about being a teenage bride, as if it was a Duke of Edinburgh's Award or something. Well, she made it and look where it landed her!"

Gwen was perched on one of the stools in front of the row of handbasins in the Ladies' at the Youth Club. The Christmas dance was at its height on the other side of the wall, and the rhythmic frenzy of Sidney and his Beat Bashers made the drops of water jump off the ends of the taps long before they were ready. She was speaking to her reflection in the mirror but what she said was aimed at Madge who was on the stool next to hers. It was a pity it happened to be Madge and not somebody more sympathetic — old Madge hadn't a clue, everyone had been staggered to see her with Eddie — but Gwen was in a talking mood and Madge would have to listen.

"It wasn't as if she hadn't lots to choose from. You remember, she went with dozens and they had style, all of them. Some of them were lovely and look what she married!" Gwen's big sister had eventually settled for a large and gentle butcher with a schoolgirl complexion. "Like something on a slab, even in the church," Gwen said. "Sacrificial." She remembered her own role as bridesmaid and brightened. "Lovely dresses we had, everyone said it was a smashing wedding."

Madge wasn't listening, just sitting with her long legs wound round each other like a kid at school. She was glowering at her reflection without trying to do anything about it. "Fancy you and Eddie!" Gwen said patronizingly, hoping to draw a confidence but failing. "And you'd better watch it, Madge, you'll get lines between your eyes if you go on frowning like that. My big sister has got lines already. I went round to their place last night — honest, it was terrible. She hadn't done a thing to her hair or her face for weeks, you could tell. Things were in such a mess, talc and fish fingers and corn plasters and nappies and Pools coupons and knitting patterns all over the place. Remember how particular she was before — if you breathed on a pair of her stockings or took a sniff of her perfume — she knew!"

"I suppose twins are like that." Madge's flat polite voice meant that her private argument concerned something else.

"You don't know how awful it was, much much worse than when we were looking after the Flints. And at least we knew it wouldn't go on till death us did part, though it seemed nearly as long."

"I've just been round there," Madge said.

"Round where?"

"To the Flints. I nipped out between dances." Madge rummaged for a clip that had got lost in the thickets of her hair.

Gwen stroked the sleek curtains that hung against either cheek. "You've got lovely hair, Madge. I mean it could be ever so nice if you'd do things with it. My big sister used to have gorgeous hair."

Gwen stared at her face in the glass. "That's what frightens me most. Nobody needs to be sorry for her. She's all right. I don't ever remember her being happy like that before, she was always narking about something. It scares me stiff the way she is now. Oh, it's nice for her, I know, but — do you think I'm really a Career Woman, Madge? I wish there was some way of being sure. I mean she hasn't been out of the house except to the launderette or the supermarket with the pram, not for weeks and weeks. Before she was married she went wild if she had to stay in two nights running. Madge — you're not listening."

"It's Sammy Flint," Madge said. "When I went round he wasn't there. Miss Harrison said she didn't know where he'd got to. He'd had his tea and then he disappeared."

On the other side of the wall the music stopped and was followed by a whirr of talk and the soft rattle of clapping. Sidney's men switched over to a new beat. "So close but miles away, you're miles away!" the music complained. Gwen said, "You'd better not keep Eddie waiting too long, it doesn't work with some."

Madge hadn't heard. "Miles away" was right. "Sammy — she thinks he nipped off when she was washing up. It wasn't Miss Harrison's fault but she was in a state." She poked bad-temperedly at her hair, not really caring.

"What you want to do is flatten it out and get rid of the frizz. You can do it on the ironing board if you use a cool iron and put on lashings of lacquer afterward," Gwen advised. "There was a piece in my magazine last week — it showed the style to choose according to what shape your face is. What shape's yours? Heart-shaped is the ideal, it says. I'm lucky, aren't I? I'm heart-shaped."

"Last Christmas he went off on his own, too. They looked and looked. In the end they found him wandering around in Dove Square."

Gwen gazed at her heart-shaped face and said, "I don't know which is worse, the dumb ones or the ones that talk. Ivor — he was the last but one — he could only talk about motorbikes. Does Eddie talk?"

"I suppose so. Yes, a bit. Sammy had gone back to where they used to live. It was when he saw the Christmas tree and the decorations in the shops."

"I mean there are other things as well as motorbikes. Why did he go back to Dove Square because of the Christmas decorations?"

"I suppose they reminded him of it, the Flints always used to go wild over Christmas, solid with balloons their place was. When did you say Mr. Flint was getting home?"

"The day after tomorrow. Christmas used to be so lovely," Gwen sighed. "I mean when we were kids and there was the Nativity Play at school. Most years I was an angel. I always wanted to be Mary but I was never chosen. What were you, Madge?"

"Back row of the shepherds, wearing a beard. I was too tall for the angels, I stuck up too far."

"You could believe anything at Christmas when you were little," Gwen said. "It was all so plain and easy and comfortable. Probably that's where Sammy's gone now — back to Dove Square."

Neither of them spoke and the tune and the shuffling feet came into their own again.

"Back to the treadmill, we can't stay out here for ever," Gwen said, yawning.

"Who's waiting for you?"

"Only Henry. Henry was always a Wise Man — terribly earnest. One year he forgot to take his glasses off. People laughed."

"He shouldn't be off on his own like that. Not at this time of night," Madge fretted. "Not Sammy Flint."

In the mirror their eyes met and kindled, recognizing a common summons. "Come on then if you're coming," Madge said, disentangling her legs and pulling the lost clip from her hair as if she were plucking poultry. "We might get a bus if we're lucky."

When Madge spoke in that voice you had about as much chance as you had against a landslide or a tidal wave. Gwen thought about her knees in their best stockings, about the unknown partners into whose eyes she might look during the next "Excuse Me," about the dreamy spell of the last waltz. "But we can't," she protested. "Eddie! Henry! We can't just go off and leave them, they'll be wild!"

"Don't be silly, they won't mind. After all, it's only us!"

Gwen's face became a mulish square. "I do mind. What's more I'm not coming. This is my last dance for ages, I'm on night duty next week. Think of it, night duty over Christmas! And I'll tell you something else, Madge, it's a pity nobody ever told you before. You're bossy, that's what. You always were bossy. Even at school you were. Ordering everyone around. The boys, too! That's why you never had one, if you want to know. I'm surprised Eddie picked on you. Everyone was surprised. Eddie, they said, Eddie and Madge, that's a bit of a giggle!"

"Well, you can tell them from me to go ahead and amuse themselves," Madge snapped, and slung her coat round her and was out through the door.

It was bitterly cold. The air smelled of frost. A few ragged shreds of snow strayed through it. She didn't have long to wait for a bus. When she had boarded it she sat hugging her own warmth, thinking about what Gwen had said and about Eddie. He'd hardly spoken a word to her tonight while they were dancing, just looked. Perhaps he thought it was a bit of a giggle, too. Perhaps the joke was over. Perhaps Gwen had been right, she knew about things. Perhaps you had to act soft with boys, like Gwen did. Well, she was blowed if she'd act soft. But she sat in the jolting bus growing colder every minute, mourning Eddie, forgetting Sammy and her errand. "Dove Square, Scarlett O'Hara!" the conductor cheeked. She froze him with a stare and alighted.

She felt her way through the blackness of the alley behind the houses. The snow had ceased but a wind caught at anything it could lay its fingers on, rattling the latches of the gates into the yards, stirring loose slates, playing drums on the lids of old rusted bins. She counted the gates. This was the entrance to Shaky's backyard. A faint tower of light was up-thrown through the nettles that grew in the area outside his basement window. So he was at home. The yard was slippery with frost; the weeds round the frozen puddle crunched as she trod on them.

As she approached the light, a shape that had been part of the solid house became separate from it and moved. Madge, swallowing her terror, cried, "Matt!"

"I don't know what you think you're doing here." Matt's voice was an angry whisper of frosted breath.

"Looking for Sammy Flint — he's run off like he did last Christmas."

"What was wrong with the dance, or did Eddie stand you up?" Matt asked nastily.

"I told you — Sammy — I'm looking for him."

"Well, you can clear off, he isn't here."

"He could be on the floor above, where they used to live. What are you doing here anyway?"

"What's wrong with my being here?"

"I only said what were you doing."

"Paying Shaky a call if you want to know."

"You weren't. You were just standing outside his

window, snooping. What were you snooping at?" She moved a step nearer. Matt blocked the way. "Look, get lost, why can't you?" he snarled. "There isn't anything to see."

Madge pushed her way past. She half-heard his little moan of anger and, "You're a fool, Madge!" Now she was close to the window and could see through into the lighted room. Yes, Shaky was there. Someone was with him.

"Matt — that man with Shaky —"

"What about him?"

"I've seen him before. He was the man who was hanging about the Flats the night we went on the swings, remember?"

"For crying out loud, Madge — I don't remember any man."

"You must remember! I thought he was coming over to speak to us but he changed his mind. I thought I knew him today when I saw him on our landing."

"Regular Sherlock," he sneered.

"No. It is the same man. I'm sure."

"So what?"

"I think he was coming away from our door. And when I went in Cousin Maudie was sitting in front of the telly laughing, just sitting there with her shoes off, laughing. 'With the compliments of the management,' she said. 'This is for you!' And she gave me the watch. Who do you suppose he is?"

"Search me, no need to go on about it. One of your Cousin Maudie's expensive pals. Go back home now.

There's nothing to stay for. I'm telling you, Madge. Clear out!"

His voice had risen sharply but there was no need for caution because voices were rising inside the room. Words came distinctly to the watchers outside the window.

"You saw where she hid it. The time she came back, you watched her. And after she'd gone away, you went and collected it."

"I don't know — anything — about any money." Shaky's poor head punctuated his words.

"That won't do, Friend Frick, that won't do at all. You see everything that goes on around here. You took it all right. The question is what did you do with it? That's the question — now for the answer. You didn't spend much of it on yourself, that's obvious. You bided your time. Yes, that's what you did, you hid the money and waited. Where did you hide it? Come on — where?" One of the dogs growled and jumped but the man's foot caught it and it lay in a corner whimpering. The other dog snarled and cowered. "Get this, Friend Frick. You can tell me where the money is here and now or you know what I can do. You wouldn't hide it in this room, you've too much sense. Somewhere around, that's where you put it. You've plenty of choice. Come on — where is it?"

Madge's fingers bit into Matt's arm. "Matt! Look! It's Sammy! Over there!"

It was Sammy. Quiet as a small domestic animal he had entered the room and was standing just inside the

door. His eyes traveled from the Salesman's face to
Shaky's and back again. They weren't scared in the ordinary sense of the word, but they shone with the fasci-
nated brilliance with which he had watched the television serial. Only now he was on the inner side of the
screen.

The Salesman had taken hold of the lapels of Shaky's
jacket and was talking close to his gray, jerking face.
"Just tell me. The money!"

The photographs on the wall looked at the two men
unmoving. But Sammy had moved. He had slipped
round the back of the room and was coming up behind
the Salesman. He was holding something in his hand.
Now he raised it.

"Sammy!" shouted Madge. "Sammy — don't! Matt,
stop him!"

What happened after that was confused. Sammy's

descending arm cut through emptiness because the Salesman had heard Madge's voice and had turned round to the window. The bottle slipped from Sammy's hand and crashed in splinters; the little dogs jumped and snarled in hysterical panic; the Salesman, whipping round again, saw Sammy standing there and made a grab for him. Matt, who had burst headlong into the room, pushed Sammy behind him and ducked to avoid the Salesman's grasping fingers. The Salesman in turn overbalanced and tripped against the oil stove. It swayed and toppled.

Every movement was arrested as the stove heeled over and fell. It seemed to fall very slowly. They were waiting for it. A moment after the crash the flame shot out along the floor like a blue arrow, then ripped upright in tongues of yellow fire. The room was filled with flames and people shouting and a confusion of movement. Madge, who had reached the bottom of the flight of steps, felt the soft bellies of the escaping dogs brush across her feet. Now the flames had attacked the curtains and were leaping up them. Someone's hand snatched at the burning fabric but it came away in fragments which scattered more flames as they fell. The oil, still seeping from the upturned stove, suddenly bloomed in fiery orange right across the floor. The room was thick with smoke. The cane back of one of the chairs crackled and burst into latticed fire.

Madge grabbed Sammy and pulled him up the steps and into the yard. "You could have killed him with that bottle! You could have killed him!" Matt brought

Shaky out; the little man was speechless with coughing. The Salesman followed.

"The Fire Brigade!" Matt shouted, "I'll go!" He was heading for the gate when the Salesman took him fast by the shoulder. "Just a minute, son!"

"Let him go!" moaned Shaky. "Everything I have is in that room!"

"And you'll have to explain to the Fire Brigade what it's doing there, won't you?" the Salesman said. "The police, too. They're bound to ask questions."

"You wouldn't! You wouldn't tell them!" Tears ran down Mr. Frick's face.

"Not what I'd do, Friend Frick. Out of my hands once the police come. You'll do any telling that has to be done. But I will do this. You say where the money is and I'll save what I can for you. Better make up your mind while there's still anything left that's worth saving."

The glass of the window cracked across; the flames were licking their way through. Smoke rose against the outer wall. The wind caught it and fanned it into flame which grew longer with each second. Sammy jumped and cheered, clapping his hands as if it were a Pantomime. Shaky wept and coughed. The little dogs crowded against the gate, jumping and scratching at it in terror, trying to find a way of escape.

The Salesman was still holding Matt captive. "Come on, Friend Frick. The money!"

"I tell you — I don't know — anything about the money!"

Something inside the room crashed and fell, then there was another crash and another. One after another Shaky's treasures were eaten by the fire. The photographs on the walls, Mrs. L'Estrange, His Majesty the King, The Reverend Robinson Crusoe, Armistice Day in Dove Square, Corporal Frick standing to attention the way the Roman sentry did in the destruction of Pompeii. All of them ashes now. The smoke from their ashes had filled the yard.

The doorway blazed a brilliant orange; they could feel the heat of it on their faces. In the windows of the floor above, light that had appeared faintly was growing steadily brighter. Gray coils of smoke seeped from the stonework.

"No use now," the Salesman said. "It's reached the floor above. You've lost the lot, Friend Frick, nobody could go in there again. Staircase and all will be gone in a moment."

The heat in the yard had become intense. Their faces were stiffened with it, their mouths and throats were filled with the reek of smoke, their eyes dried up and dazzled. They backed against the gate and stood watching.

From inside the house came a tremendous prolonged crash — flame spurted, sparks flew up high into the night sky, one of the window frames on the upper floor ignited.

"That's it," the Salesman said. "That's the staircase."

Sammy was jabbering and pointing. It was impossible to translate what he said. One word appeared to be

repeated time and again. It sounded like "Money —
money — money!"

"What's he saying?" the Salesman demanded.
"Money? Is that it? Who understands this jabbering
baby?"

"I do," Madge said.

"Then get him to talk sense."

"He is."

"What did he say?"

The flames made a moving pattern across Madge's
face. Her voice was ice cold.

"He used to come here to play. One day he saw the
lady. He followed her. He watched what she did."

"Go on then — what did she do?"

"He says she went upstairs in one of the houses and
moved the lino away and took out some money from
below the floor."

"And after that?"

"She held the money in her hand for a long time and
then she put it back again, where she'd got it."

"And then —"

"After she'd gone he went and lifted the board and
took the money out."

"And then? Go on!"

"He took it to the house where he used to live and
hid it in his own secret hiding place."

The Salesman's voice was uneven. "Where was his
secret hiding place?"

"Under the tread of one of the stairs. There was a
loose board."

"Yes, but which house — which house?"

"This one." Madge pointed straight into the blaze.

The Salesman's long tearing sigh was audible above the noise of the flames. "That's the truth, is it? That's what he said?"

"Yes."

"I could have done things with that money." Whoever the Salesman was talking to, it was to none of them. "I knew it was my last chance. I had that much sense. I could have done things." He turned away from the heat and glare.

Madge asked, "Was it Cousin Maudie who hid the money?"

The man wheeled round and stared at her. " 'Cousin Maudie?' So that's what she taught you to call her, is it?"

Madge nodded.

"Well, I don't blame her," he said. He looked at Madge for another full minute. Neither of them spoke. Then he made for the gate and lifted the latch and was gone. They heard his footsteps in the alley. Now he had reached the street.

When the sound of his tread had completely faded, Matt said, "Come on then," and shepherded them through the gate. They were a dazed and ragged crew. They followed Matt out into the Square and walked in silence to the front of the houses. Here they could see that the fire was gaining ground. Smoke belched from the hall door and the broken fanlight. Soon the whole of the house and its neighbors would be alight. They halted for a moment and watched it. Sammy had begun to cry. He clamored at Madge for comfort but she didn't seem to see or hear him. Shaky stood with humped shoulders and sagging knees, like an old man, no trace at all of the brisk Corporal Frick. The little dogs ran round his feet unheeded. Matt realized that whether he wanted it or not he was now in charge.

A long way off a fire engine wailed. It was coming closer. Some passing driver must have spotted the fire and had given the alarm. Soon the authorities would be here to save anything that was worth saving.

"We'll move away before anyone arrives and asks questions," Matt said. "Stop crying, Sammy, it's all over now. Take Mr. Frick's hand, he'll come home with us. We'll stick to the back streets, I know the way. It's quite a distance, but no use standing around waiting on the chance of a bus. Better no one sees us anyway. You and Mr. Frick go ahead. Cross the road and turn down past the old sweet shop. We'll catch up."

Sammy took Corporal Frick's hand and they did as Matt bade them. Madge was the last to come. She came slowly. Matt waited for her. She didn't say anything, didn't look at him.

For the first time in his life he knew how separate people were from each other, so that you couldn't know or even try to guess what someone else was feeling. You couldn't share it. He ached for something to say to her. There must be something.

"Come on," he said as she drew level. "We'd better get a move on, it's late. My mum will be wild. So'll yours."

↬ 10 ↫

BEFORE there was any hint of daylight the sky above the rooftops was rocked by the voices of early bells, and it wasn't until long after they had stopped ringing that the morning of Christmas dawned, pale and unobserved. There was no traffic astir except for an occasional empty bus or a trundling milk float. A wafer-faced moon dipped and disappeared. She had completed her escort duty; the star had dawned in the East; the herald angels had been dismissed. Christmas was now.

Matt, dawdling outside the Flats and stamping to keep his feet warm, felt bored and a little cheated. Sometimes it was like this with Christmas, as if after a hard journey you arrived at last at the top of the hill and there was nothing there, or at least it wasn't as momentous as you had expected. The whole city had been in the Christmas procession for weeks, fanfares from the Salvation Army's brass band at each street corner, three times the ordinary number of letters arriving by every post, soloists for the "Messiah" on all the notice boards, Christmas fairs galore, shopwindows bright with synthetic frost or veiled by strings of pink sausages and the feathered necks of poultry hanging upside down, a bombardment of carols on the radio for as long as you could remember, the pavement outside the greengrocer's bristling with Christmas trees, a tightening excitement as the number of shopping days lessened and purses grew thinner, a last frantic harvest home of bread and vegetables, a final closing of doors. The lights in the windows all over the city went out. And next morning it was Christmas.

The Christmas tree outside the Flats had taken punishment in the high winds of a couple of days ago. Some of the streamers had come unmoored and the silver swags were tangled. A joker had stuck branches of berried holly into the earholes of the piece of modern sculpture, giving it a jaunty and confused appearance.

After "Christians Awake" and breakfast, Matt presented his mother with the box he had bought for her at the chemist's — talcum powder, two tablets of toilet soap, four bath cubes, some hand cream, all secured in plastic with silver bows. "Geranium!" she exclaimed, reading the label. "How lovely, Matt. Really, you shouldn't!" And he admired his new leather gloves in which this year the tips of his fingers reached right to the end. They smelled the way new gloves should smell, and the press button at his wrist made a satisfying click when he pressed it shut. "Smashing, Mum," he said. There was a diary as well, with a pencil and a ribbon marker. He filled in as much of the personal detail as he could, even the space "In case of accident please inform . . ." This gave him an important and pleasurably fatalistic feeling.

He thought his mother looked tired and a little sad,

and tried not to notice. It might be his fault. Yesterday they had taken the bus into the country, to the village where they had lived seven years before. Every Christmas Eve his mother made the journey, Mr. Ricardo always gave her the day off. "I'll come with you this year," Matt suggested. "No dear, there's no need — really." "But I'd like to come."

All the way in the bus she nursed the holly wreath on her knee, sometimes pressing her fingers against the prickles. "Will I take it for you now, Mum?" "No dear, it's all right." They got off the bus and she carried it up the hill. The countryside was bare and lacked color. There were plenty of holly wreaths on other graves in the churchyard. Matt read his father's name on the stone and felt at a loss, not knowing what to say or if he should say anything. He had never learned how to mourn. His mother had been so brave, so cheerful. He felt she should have taught him how to mourn.

He stood a little behind her watching her frosty breath quicken. Birds chattered incessantly from the thick thorn hedge that arched above the gate, and on the hillside beyond the sheep were never silent. His mother took his arm as they walked away. "You can't hear the stream," she said. "It must be frozen up."

While they waited for the return bus she took a thermos from her carrier bag and they drank coffee, wrapping their chilled hands round the mugs. In the bus she produced sandwiches and talked all the time, so that the mission became a party.

"That was where your grandfather lived, Matt. I

remember the first time your Father took me there — that tree at the corner of the orchard, it was always the first of all the trees, your father used to say — cowslips, that was the field for cowslips — you can imagine what this hill was like with the pram, Matt — that was your aunt's house, your Aunt Harriet where the silver teapot came from, she was your father's youngest sister, his favorite, if you had been a girl you were to be Harriet — and that was where the dance was held where I met your father. Think of it, Matt, he hadn't intended to go, but one of Tom's boys (that was your Uncle Tom over the mantelpiece, you have quite a look of him about the eyes people always said), he sprained his ankle and so your father came to the dance instead."

As she talked she glanced sideways at him, inviting him to share the past with her, but he sat glum and silent, hating himself and wishing she would stop talking or that he could conjure up a little space around himself in which he could be private. His mother was labeling him, fastening chains round him, so that everything he was he owed to people in the past, or else to chance. Think of it — he might have been Harriet! He might have been the son of some other man if Uncle Tom's son hadn't sprained his ankle. There was nothing special or unique in being himself. With his uncle's eyes he was looking at his father's tree. He was a sort of haphazard Indentikit, a secondhand person, that was what it worked out at.

"You said you wanted to come, Matt," his mother said in a puzzled voice.

"Yes, I know. I did want to come."

"I told you there was no need."

"But I wanted to. Anyway why didn't we go and see some of these relations? We'd have had time."

"You can't push yourself at people," she said. "And don't make crumbs all over the bus, Matt. The conductor won't like it."

When they got back to the Happy Land his mother went into the stationer's to buy another Christmas card — someone had sent her an unexpected one and she must retaliate before the last post was collected — and while he waited for her Madge came by on her way home. He hadn't seen Madge since the night of the fire. After they had turned their backs on Dove Square she went straight home while he took Sammy back to the Flints' flat, and lodged Mr. Frick with a cousin of Mr. Ricardo's who had a spare room and a warm heart and wouldn't talk. The little dogs he had left at a boarding kennels. He wondered if Madge would be different.

She wasn't. "See you tomorrow morning — meet you at the Christmas tree," she directed. "I'll bring the presents. And be sure you're early."

So here he was waiting for her on Christmas morning, trying to keep warm and feeling a little bleak. He cheered himself by thinking how pleased and grateful the Flint tribe would be with the presents and how much he would enjoy being benevolent. He might even pat a few fair-haired heads, forgetting how much he'd ached to knock them together a couple of weeks back. But he wished Madge would get a move on. Early, she'd said. There was no one about, the pavements of the Happy Land were empty. Everyone was indoors. Few curtains had yet been parted and the windows shone like rows of brilliantly colored postage stamps. Inside each of these windows a private Christmas had begun, yards and yards of holly paper ripped open, tinsel bows untied, secrets exploded, hearts' desires fulfilled, stockings held up by their toes and shaken.

Henry came and stood beside him, stamping and blowing on his hands. He asked, "What your joyful news today? Give me one guess — you got a diary. You haven't seen Gwen about, have you?"

"No. Anyway she's on night duty."

"I know she is, clot. She comes off at eight. I only asked if you'd seen her."

"I told you I haven't."

"Not much comfort and joy about you, old son, is there? What's up anyway?"

"Nothing."

"That was a fine old blaze they had in Dove Square the other evening; pity we missed it. Did you read about it in the papers?"

"Yes."

"If it got as far as all those feathers we spread around it can't have half stunk. Shaky's staying with Mr. Ricardo's cousin but nobody's supposed to know."

"Is he?" Matt said noncommittally.

"Poor old Shaky! Here's Gwen now. How beautiful upon the mountains!"

Gwen looked about twelve, her face was pink and

radiant, her cap crooked, her hair stuck out in a messy halo. She didn't notice the boys until Henry said "Hiya!" She was walking on clouds, the pavement wasn't necessary.

"Oh Henry! Oh Matt! Happy Christmas!" she exclaimed, and stood yawning rapturously. "Gosh, I'm sleepy!"

Henry asked, "You look pleased with yourself, anyway. What's so wonderful?"

"Christmas!" she said. "I was on duty in the Delivery Room and just when all the bells began to ring the baby was born!"

Henry fumbled in his pocket and produced a little packet. "It's for you. Happy Christmas." He waited for her to open it, standing with the pleased expression of an expectant dog.

Gwen took the package and slid it into the pocket of her coat without even looking. It could have been a pearl necklace or a bar of chocolate. "Oh, Henry! Oh, thank you! How terribly kind of you! Isn't Christmas just gorgeous! The bells were banging away and the baby was bawling, it was perfect," and she drifted off home, already more than half asleep.

"Let nothing you dismay," Henry said heavily. "If it had been a couple of sardines in an envelope she'd have been bound to notice."

"What was it?"

"Perfume. French. The man said it meant 'I'm coming back.' Never mind, there's a Boxing Night Carnival at the ice rink tomorrow, bound to be plenty of birds there. What about coming?"

"No. Thanks all the same."

"Well, God rest you merry, anyway."

After Henry had taken himself off Madge arrived. She brought the bag full of presents. "Happy Christmas, Matt," she said, not giving him time to say anything. "I've tied them all up and written their names on the labels. Will we go on up right away? It must be pretty dreary for them, not much of a Christmas with her still away. But they've got the decorations up, balloons, I saw them in the window. It's a good thing Pa Flint's home anyway."

He wanted to ask why she minded so much about the Flints and so little about herself but her face forbade questions.

They crossed the grass and had almost reached the block where the Flints' flat was when a bus rounded the corner and drew in to the stop. A woman got out. When the bus had gone she started to walk toward them. Madge stood still, staring.

"Come on, then," Matt urged. "No use hanging about here — I'm perished. You were late."

"Wait a minute Matt. Don't you see who it is?"

"Who who is?" He looked and saw who it was. There could be no mistaking her, it was Ma Flint. She didn't look any different from usual, no hint of embarrassment or drama or distress. She carried an umbrella and a shopping bag. She might have been out doing the messages. Now she was coming home.

They dodged quickly into the entry of one of the shops. "Don't let her see us." They stood waiting. Ma Flint walked past and went unhurried into the block.

"She's come back!"

They waited long enough to allow Ma Flint time to enter the lift, then they followed warily as far as the entrance hall. The ropes of the lift were still moving, now they stopped, the lift door was opening on an upper floor.

"What do you suppose will happen now?"

"What do you mean — what'll happen?" Madge's voice was scornful. "She's come back, that's all."

"Did they know she was coming?"

"I called in yesterday. They'd have told me if they did."

"She can't just roll up like that," Matt objected.

"Why not? Anyway she has."

"But — well, I mean — walking out on them and then walking in again when it suits her!"

"I can't see what's stopping her."

Nothing was stopping her. High overhead a door had been opened. There was a moment of utter silence. Then even from the ground floor they could hear the roar of the welcome home, the shouting, the cries of surprise, the laughter, the cheers, the stamping. Ma Flint was restored to the bosom of her family. The noise of reunion continued for a long time. At last the door closed again and the uproar dwindled into a private riot.

Matt was outraged. "I ask you! Treating them all the way she did and then turning up because she feels like it."

Madge sighed and said, "They felt like it too, by the sound of it. Now what do you suppose we do with this little lot?" She fingered the carefully labeled parcels a trifle contemptuously.

"We can't take them up. Not now."

"Of course we can't." Madge sounded bleak but positive.

"I suppose we could just dump them at the door for them to find when they come out."

"Yes. That's what we'll have to do."

Madge fished in her pocket and produced a pen. She wrote "Happy Christmas from Two Well-Wishers" and they went stealthily up in the lift and built the parcels into a pile outside the Flints' front door. It was still vibrating.

Coming down in the lift again, feeling flat and cheated, Matt said, "All the same it isn't right!"

"Oh Matt, you do go on!"

"What do you suppose Pa Flint did when they opened the door?"

"What did you want him to do? Clout her or something? Either he's glad to see her or he's not. He was glad."

Dissatisfied, he stared at the succession of floors rising and disappearing. "What would *she* do if *he* came back?" he asked. Names were impossible but the question was necessary.

"He won't. It was the money he came for."

"But if he did — ?"

"They'd have to work it out some way, I suppose."

They reached the ground floor. "May as well get back then," Matt said without moving. "Not long till dinner," he said, wondering why he didn't feel hungry.

"My mum was cooking like crazy when I came out,"

Madge said. To his surprise she sounded pleased and even a little proud. A couple of days ago Cousin Maudie cooking would have been a cue for a bit of a laugh — Cousin Maudie trailing her silk dressing gown through the gravy, dropping her eyelashes into the sprouts and cigarette ash among the chips. But that particular joke was over for good and all. It might take a bit of getting used to, but he was grateful, from the bottom of his heart.

They left the lift and when they were out on the grass again they looked back to the windows of the Flints' flat. Even here the sounds of celebration reached them. There was a movement at the window, a pane had been opened. Madge cried, "Oh, look!" and pointed. High up in the air a red balloon had appeared. It looked the size of a holly berry. It hung a moment, then made a majestic descent, hesitating, swooping — and finally it reached the ground and bobbed about, trailing its thread. Madge ran and picked it up. Cheers from above greeted this. Arms were waving out of the window, voices calling. Madge and Matt stood and waved back. Now a second balloon, a blue one, followed the first and reached the grass. Matt claimed this as his. They brandished balloons and shouted and capered. There were final cheers and the window was closed.

"Gosh I'm hungry!" Matt said, discovering that he was. "I'm going to call at the kennels when I've had my dinner, to take Shaky's little dogs up on the Downs for a walk."

"What's going to happen to Shaky?"

"He'll be all right. He's having Christmas dinner with Miss Harrison."

"Is he? Do you think there's anything on there?"

"What do you mean? Anything on?"

"R-r-romance!"

"Don't be a nit, Madge, Miss Harrison's old, they're both old."

"Like we'll be some day."

"Old? Us?"

"Like this." She sucked in her mouth and pinched her cheeks into pouches below her eyes.

Matt thought of the clean pages in the diary, and the clean pages in all the other diaries, year after year after year. "Not for ages we won't," he said. "You could come if you like, I mean with me and the dogs."

"Oh, all right," she said.

"Half past two. And mind you're not late."

She made a face at him. He walked back to his own block of flats. As he passed the Christmas tree he twisted the thread of his balloon round one of the branches and left it there. It was an act of homage. The Christmas tree blazed at him and took its place in the procession of memorable Christmas trees.

When he entered the hall the lift was waiting as if it had been expecting him, but he ignored it and whistled his way up nine flights of stairs.

364721